'So compelling ... dar[k] account of a girl b[ecoming a woman.]'
HOT PRESS

'Recalling the grotesque of Christine Schutt and
Deborah Levy, Susannah Dickey's *Tennis Lessons* is an
achingly vital novel, a work of blood and flesh,
convulsing in the heat of mortality.'
KEVIN BREATHNACH

'Revitalising ... following a young woman slaloming
wildly on a potholed road to adulthood. The spirit and
taut wit of the protagonist flexes and twitches on every
page. I couldn't put it down, and savoured
every propulsively odd turn.'
DAZED

Tennis Lessons

SUSANNAH DICKEY

BLACK SWAN

TRANSWORLD PUBLISHERS
Penguin Random House, One Embassy Gardens,
8 Viaduct Gardens, London SW 11 7BW
www.penguin.co.uk

Transworld is part of the Penguin Random House group of companies
whose addresses can be found at global.penguinrandomhouse.com

Penguin
Random House
UK

First published in Great Britain in 2020 by Doubleday
an imprint of Transworld Publishers
Black Swan edition published 2021

A CIP catalogue record for this book
is available from the British Library.

ISBN
9781784165055

Typeset in Bembo Std by Jouve (UK), Milton Keynes.
Printed and bound in Great Britain by Clays Ltd, Elcograf S.p.A.

The authorized representative in the EEA is Penguin Random House Ireland,
Morrison Chambers, 32 Nassau Street, Dublin D02 YH68.

Penguin Random House is committed to a sustainable
future for our business, our readers and our planet. This book
is made from Forest Stewardship Council® certified paper.

For my family

Prologue

Throughout your life you dream about an antique see-saw. You never see it – the you in the dream is sightless – but you know what it looks like, all rusted iron and worn wood, and you can hear it, creaking in the dark. It tips on its pivot independently of a person, and there's a wailing sound, like a high-pitched police siren, accompanying its movements. You are stuck fast in the blackness and you can hear the steady thud as each end collides with the ground and the growing intensity of its scream. Eventually the sound seems to be coming from inside your skull.

As a child you would wake from the dream sweaty and breathless, the sheets bunched into damp creases in your hands. You would run into your mother's room and she would be alert by the time you reached her bedside. She would kiss your head and rock you back and forth. Your father wouldn't be there – he'd be asleep in the spare bedroom across the landing. The first few times this happened you asked why, and your mother said, 'He's only sleeping in there because he has a cold and I can't afford to get sick at the moment.' As you get older your mother can't afford to get sick more and more frequently, and the fifth or sixth time you refer to it as 'Dad's room' she does not correct you.

Eventually you learn to stop waking her – you never

learn how to explain what the dream is about. Instead you stay in bed and try to make sense of your room in the dark: the black blobs of the wardrobe, the wicker chair, the soft toys. The siren fades and swells in your ears.

PART I

PART III

Three years old – May

You have an enormous rag doll named Frangipane. She has a round, flat face like a whoopee cushion, and hair made of individually sewn-in strands of brown thread, the same shade as yours. Her smile is a thin, U-shaped capillary, and she wears a yellow dress patterned with sunflowers. You adore her. One day you are sitting on the pink rug in your bedroom, twirling her boneless legs around one another. You are also dressed in yellow, and you love that you and Frangipane match. Your mother is sitting on the edge of your bed. She gives all your toys difficult names and then teaches you to sound them out, one syllable at a time.

The doorbell sounds and she presses her hands down on her thin knees and pushes herself up from the mattress. When she's gone you fold Frangipane in two until her permanently shoed feet find a home among her hair. You hear the door close and your mother's steps fade as she walks down the hall. You go to the top of the stairs and wait, the doll still contorted in your hands like a briefcase. When your mother emerges from the kitchen, you throw Frangipane. She hits the carpet about a third of the way and tumbles down the rest of the stairs. Your mother, occupied with a letter, jerks her head up, sees the flailing child-sized blur of yellow-clad limbs and brown hair. She careens down the hall, collapses like a clothes horse at the bottom of the staircase. She grips Frangipane in one hand. She stares up at you.

Four years old – March

You are sitting on a carpeted floor in an empty room. There are gloomy, furniture-shaped ghosts on the carpet, marking the spots where the sofa, the armchair, the table used to be. The rest of the carpet is faded by sunlight to the colour of nausea. Only the TV remains; it's squat and chunky with a huge protuberance out its back, like a skull. *The Animals of Farthing Wood* is on. Outside, your mother and father are packing the car full of lamps and end tables and boxes of books. The van that had your bed in it has already left – you watched it go with your face pressed against the window, and when you asked your father, 'Will I ever see it again?' he laughed so aggressively he dropped a stack of shoeboxes and your mother shouted 'Careful!' from the kitchen. On screen, Whistler the heron is carrying a toad in his mouth across a motorway. Your parents are arguing – he carried a large chest of drawers downstairs without waiting for her to help him.

'What use will you be if you destroy your back lifting things that are far too heavy? Could you at least try to be helpful?'

Your father says nothing.

'The smaller animals don't stand a chance,' Vixen says to Fox.

Your father continues to play Tetris with the car's contents, flattening coats with his hand while squeezing boxes in on top.

'Kestrel and Owl could carry them over?' Fox suggests, and Vixen replies, 'Yes, but they're natural enemies!'

When the house is emptied you are put in a booster seat in the back of the car, next to a cardboard box with a picture of a toaster on it that is now inhabited by a kettle. On the drive to the new house you look out of the window at the grassy roadside verges. You think about two hedgehogs, flattened under the wheels of a truck.

Five years old – July

An objectionably sunny day spent in a bathroom showroom. Your mother and grandmother – your only living grandparent – are debating the merits of a chrome finish and you have used up the hours gliding between the rows of toilet seats, stroking the plastic and ceramic and wood. You opted mentally for either the clear plastic, pocked with fusilli-shaped twists of barbed wire, or the one with bubbles and yellow and blue and green fish. Finally, after choosing a single-level mixer tap, your mother selects the ashy-blue toilet seat. It has an artificial tree-bark pattern: etched lines broken up by painted-on knolls. The oddness of the simulacrum makes you wonder if you're supposed to feel like an animal, shitting in the woods.

On the walk back to the car you decide to say, loudly, 'I don't like the one we got. I think it's disgusting,' because 'disgusting' is a word you have learned to use with confidence only recently, and because unsolicited honesty is something you are still trying out. Your mother heaves a sigh that seems to travel the length of the car park. In a tired voice she says, 'You know, part of being grown up is learning when to keep things to yourself.'

You sleep on the way home, your head trapped in a triangle of sunlight and your neck bent like a crowbar. You are lodged between your grandmother and the white cardboard box printed with the showroom logo. The box looks like it ought to have a birthday cake inside. All three of you – your increasingly deaf grandmother, the toilet seat, you – are wearing seat belts.

Six years old – October

'Can you spell it, though?'

'H-O-S-P-I-T-A-L.'

'Clever girl.'

This is how you like your mother best. She seems most relaxed when she's driving, and she seems to like you best when you're learning new words. A muffled ringing noise comes from her handbag. She mutters, 'Blast,' and then twists in her seat to show you her exaggerated-guilt face. You laugh. She pulls into a layby and scrabbles for her phone. Her blonde hair is in two shoulder-length plaits, thin as fingers. She answers the phone, 'Hi, Joan,' and you chew on the straw of your Ribena carton and swing your feet. She says, 'Uh huh. Uh huh. Yeah. No – no problem,

Joan. I hope it's all OK. Uh huh. Bye-bye.' She hangs up the phone and sighs.

'What's wrong?'

'Oh – Joan's son has ended things with his fiancée, Molly, for the second time and apparently it's all just so desperately urgent that Joan can't attend the fundraiser tonight.'

'Fiancée?'

'Yes, it means they were going to get married. It's F-I-A-N-C-E-E. Two E's because she's female, and the first E has a little line over it.'

'Is he sad?'

'Apparently so.'

'Is he . . .' and you pause, and a word appears in your mind. You think hard, '. . . unmollified?'

Your mother doesn't say anything for a moment. She peers at you. 'Where did you learn that word?'

'Dictionary.'

She laughs. It sounds like a wind chime. She shakes her head. 'That was very clever.'

You feel so happy you might burst.

Seven years old – August

The guinea pig's eyes are like two droplets of oil. It watches you from behind a thick, translucent pane of plastic. You are inside an enormous structure made of pale-yellow tubes. Every so often one of the tubes opens into an area with a small circular window that looks into a guinea pig enclosure. Inside the structure is as bright and cosy as an incubator.

You can hear the muffled noises of families outside, negotiating lunch orders and sitting at picnic tables. You had a burger for lunch. Your father ate your tomato and lettuce and your mother let you leave the table once you had eaten all the meat. You sit cross-legged and observe the guinea pig. Its nose wiggles at you.

'Guinea pigs are really stupid, you know.'

The suddenness of the voice unbalances you. A boy emerges from one of the tubes. He is big – both tall and chubby – and he takes up an enormous amount of what had felt a moment ago like your own private chamber. You stare at him.

'They just eat and poo and get sick. My dad told me. Then they get stuck in places and they die. They're so stupid.'

The boy has a ketchup stain down the front of his yellow t-shirt. His hair is shaven and his cheeks are round and pink. You turn back to the guinea pig. You look at the crescents of shine on each of its black eyes. Its fur is soft-looking, pale brown with white patches. Its nose never stops wobbling.

The boy continues. 'My dad had two when he was little and one got stuck in a chest of drawers and they only found it when it started to smell. Stupid, ugly rat-things.'

You imagine holding the guinea pig on your lap and stroking its drooping ears and feeding it batons of celery and carrot. You sense that it might like that too.

'Hey. Aren't you going to say anything?'

You turn reluctantly back to the boy. He's frowning at you. Yesterday you watched your video of *The Little Mermaid* for the eighth time. You think of one particular scene.

You tap your throat with your hand, the way Ariel does when Eric starts asking her questions. The boy says, 'What?' and you tap your throat more fervently. You shake your head and make a 'No' gesture with your hands. You tap your throat. The 'No' gesture. You tap your throat. The boy looks uncertain.

'You can't talk?'

You shake your head again. His mouth sits open. He breaks eye contact. He gives the guinea pig another disgusted glance and then he clambers back into the tube. You turn back to the window into the enclosure. The guinea pig has not moved. You say, 'Sorry about that,' and the two of you resume looking at one another until you hear your father calling for you.

Eight years old – June

'Would you ever sit down, pal? Stop fussing and cool your jets. Here' – he pours a generous measure of coffee-flavoured liqueur into your mother's glass – 'get liquored up.'

'Whoa – that's enough!' she says, batting him away, but it's not a real gesture, you can tell – the arc of her hand has no edges, is loose and inviting. Your mother is more like a rag doll when her twin brother is around; she is malleable, easily coaxed into some posture of relaxation. Your father comes in from the garden, his arms full of air-dried laundry. Your uncle bows his head in reverence, says in a nasal, aristocratic voice, 'Ah, the man of the house, shall thee have a drink?'

'He needs to drive you to the station later, remember?' your mother says, smiling, but still eyeing her mug warily.

'Prithee do not hampen these joyful tidings, wench,' your uncle says, and he spreads his fingers and places his entire hand over her face. Her laughter behind his palm is muffled.

'Go on then, mate,' your father says, setting the laundry on the counter and sitting down next to you. 'Just a smidge.'

Your uncle pours another three-inch measure into a glass. You bite on the knuckle of your finger and titter.

'Ah, and what about for the wee birthday bairn?' he says, now in parody-Glaswegian, and he hovers the bottle over your glass of milk. You look at your mother imploringly.

'A tiny bit,' she says. 'And I mean that − a tiny bit.'

'Oh, but she is so gracious in her reign. How blessèd are we to have her.' Your uncle flicks the bottle and a mahogany raindrop spreads across the white surface. You take a sip, and your mouth fills with sweet and smoky, chocolate and salt. You lick your lips.

'Oh no, she's got a taste for it,' your father says, and you are surprised when your mother laughs.

'She's a sophisticated woman now, no doubt about it,' your uncle says, and he too-loudly claps his glass against your mother's. She laughs again, your father joins in, and your uncle gives you a vaudeville wink. You think he is the best person in the world.

Eight years old – August

The screen cuts from the commercial break back to the group of people marooned on an island. You reach into the bag of marshmallows in your father's hand and take three: one pink, two white. You wad them, one by one, into your mouth. The sky outside is ripening as the sun sets. Your mother is at her weekly church women's group, and it is during this time that your father allows you to watch the programmes and films deemed trashy or unsuitable by your mother. It's your shared secret, and you like that even in the moments when you are not watching television the two of you have this illicit lingua franca of pop culture.

Last week on this series a man was sucked into the slowly rotating engine of a broken plane. His body was made rapidly, gruesomely, into grass cuttings. Your father twitched in his seat, said, 'Whoa!' before breaking into nervous laughter. He smiled at you, embarrassed, said, 'Was that a bit scary? Should I turn it off?' You shook your head vehemently.

This week there is an injured man in a tent. A blonde woman straddles him in her khaki shorts, checks his abdomen for places of tenderness. He exhales when she presses down, his breath wheezing like a fire bellows. His eyes are locked on her, and the moment seems so intimate you feel like an intruder. You angle your eyes to the right. Your father's embarrassed expression is a mirror image of your own. The bag of marshmallows goes neglected as the two of you become co-conspirators – reluctant voyeurs to this soft skin-on-skin encounter.

Eight years old – March

'Maybe try not to say anything that'll upset her, OK?'

'OK.'

You look at your father's head from the back seat. The thinning brown hair and the red scalp. Your skin feels stiff and smells like chlorine. There was a plaster floating on the surface of the pool; it had a few dark hairs and a cube of skin attached to it. It made you feel queasy, and while the other children practised the arm motions for breaststroke you kept your eyes on the plaster and tried not to gag.

Your mother is sitting at the kitchen table when you walk in. She's wearing her pale-blue dressing gown and her hair hangs in strings around her face. Lined up in front of her on the table are three tablets. She's a receptionist in a private dental clinic, but she hasn't been to work in two weeks. The day before, you came home from school to find all your stuffed toys in a bin liner at the top of the stairs. 'This house is a pigsty,' she shouted at the walls, at you. 'We have far too much junk.' As she slammed downstairs and into the kitchen you quietly and methodically replaced the animals on the shelves, apologizing to the monkey, the bear, the other bear.

You think you want to punish her, for what she did to the animals, for being in a dressing gown at twelve o'clock, for making the air in the house feel tight. She smiles at you.

'How was swimming?'

You grip your swim bag in your hands and feel wetness seep through the fabric – you hadn't wrung out your suit properly. This will annoy her. You drop the bag on to the floor and it makes a noise like a cooked tomato, bursting. Dampness pools out from underneath it. You say nothing.

Nine years old – October

'Dad?'

'Hmmm?'

He is lying outstretched on the grey-blue carpet of his bedroom floor. His t-shirt is stretched tight across his belly. Sunday afternoons are always like this, lazy and lilting. You sit down next to him. He was asleep when you walked in.

'If you could get shot anywhere, where would it be?'

'What's that?'

'If you had to get shot.'

'Eh?'

'Where would you get shot?'

'On the beach might be nice.'

'No, where on your body?'

'Huh?'

You decide to help him.

'I think I would get shot in the shoulder, or the hand, maybe.'

'If you got shot in the hand it would probably need to be cut off.'

'Oh.'

You pull at a loose thread of rubber on the sole of one of

his wilting slippers. He scratches at the inch of hairy skin between the bottom of his t-shirt and the top of his trousers. He contemplates the ceiling.

'I might just go with the head.'

'But you'd die.'

'Yeah, but it'd be quick and painless, which lots of deaths aren't. Plus, I wouldn't have to deal with the pain of getting shot somewhere else.'

'That's really silly.'

'I promise to give it some more thought in case it ever comes up.'

'Mum?'

'Yes?'

She is sitting at the kitchen table, transferring contacts from her old address book to her new address book, which has a painting of people in a park on the cover.

'If you could get shot anywhere, where would it be?'

She half smiles – it looks involuntary.

'If I were to be shot I doubt I would get given the choice.'

'But if you were.'

The half-smile goes. She looks at the wall.

'In this country it has always tended to be head or legs, although again, people don't usually get given the choice.'

'So would you go with legs?'

'I don't know. I'm trying to concentrate.'

'Dad said head, so he wouldn't have to deal with the pain of getting shot somewhere else.'

Your mother sighs and sets her pen down. She has seemed, if not happier, recently, then more placid, and it occurs to you now that you might be threatening that.

'I suppose in this dream scenario your father wouldn't have responsibilities or dependants.' She pauses. 'Or maybe he would, and that's the point.'

'I think I'd go with hand, or shoulder.'

'Your hand would have to be amputated.'

'I guess, but it'd be better than just dying.'

The address book has lettered tabs that form a tiny staircase along the pages' edge.

A–B

B–C

C–D

D–E

You lean over and walk your fingertips down the staircase. Your mother watches you.

'The nice thing about being a little older, and being a Christian, is you don't worry about death as much.'

'But Dad's not a Christian.'

Another pause. 'No, he's not.'

'How do you know which B names to put in the A–B section and which to put in B–C?'

'I suppose you do it by the second letter.'

'What happens if you know too many people with "B–u" surnames and you run out of space in B–C?'

'I don't know. I don't know too many people with "B–u" surnames so I doubt it will ever come up.'

'Are you worried about running out of space for any of the sections?'

'I don't know that many people. I expect the book will remain largely empty, OK?'

'OK.'

Your mother's hand hovers over the pen.

'If you had to choose between me being shot or me having to go to a labour camp, which would you pick?'

'Why on earth would you ask that?'

'I saw it in a film.'

She rolls her eyes upwards, to where your father is sleeping on the floor. You can see the red rim below the white.

'I suppose it might depend on how much I thought you would suffer. If there was very little chance of your surviving, I might rather you had an easy and painless death.'

'Do you think I could survive a labour camp?'

She laughs and picks up the pen between two thin fingers. She was born without a finger on her left hand, but instead of a gap where the finger ought to be her whole hand is just narrower, her palm the same width as her wrist.

'I don't know, darling. Being shot might be the kinder thing.'

You leave the kitchen, disappointed. You wonder how you might go about changing her mind.

Nine years old – February 14th

You are in a room full of long people dressed in black. Your skirt is burgundy and made of heavy corduroy. It's covered in tiny multicoloured blossoms. From a distance you wonder if the flowers look like insects, and you're worried that the anarchy of your skirt is dominating the room, that everyone is too afraid to look at you. You sit, stiff, on the dark-grey sofa, gaudy as a beacon. You're scared to move in case you startle the tall, black flamingoes. You wish you were wearing black too, but your mother said, as she laid out your outfit yesterday afternoon, 'Black is too stark for a child. It's not appropriate.' Then she went back to bed.

You dig your nails into the rivulets of the fabric; you imagine them puncturing the dents in the skirt and digging into the skin, turning you into strips. The sofa is leather, and every movement elicits a low-pitched squeak, and it's funny but you can't laugh, in your carnival skirt and your furry boots. You count the flowers on your thighs:

Three yellow – you hear the raspy sobs of your deaf grandmother, wet and messy and impossible to ignore.

Six blue – your father, setting down a tumbler of red wine, lowers himself shakily to his knees and places his hand on the carpet. He puts his other hand, sweaty and curled like a baseball mitt, on your knee. He half whispers, 'Always tell someone if you're feeling scared.' His voice is slurred and you stare at him – you wonder if he is entitled to this sloppy, public grief. His breath smells like vinegar and egg and you stop inhaling until he has straightened up. His hand is still using your knee as a balustrade. He retrieves his wine and a fat drop plops on to your lap.

Twelve pink – someone asks where your mother is.

Three white – she's having a lie-down.

Four green – a squeak as you distribute weight from one hip to the other.

Another yellow – you struggle to separate one ham sandwich from its neighbour when a plate is passed around. You bite into it and your teeth immediately discover resistance. Your tongue nudges its way around a lump of gristle and a wave of nausea moves through you. You put your fingers to your mouth and remove the knot. You glance around to make sure no one is looking, and while making a show of scratching your thigh you secrete the gristle into the gap between two sofa cushions. You stand up.

In the study-turned-sepulchre, his old study, the light casts a yellow glow on to your uncle's cheeks. He has the same features as your mother – the same sharp nose and high cheekbones – but they always looked different on him. He travelled a lot, and in the photos he would send – of him standing next to the Parthenon or at a Christmas market in Germany – he always looked like he'd been designed and constructed using nothing but straight lines. His nickname for your mother was 'Squishy', or sometimes 'Squishter' – an amalgam of 'sister' and 'squish' that delighted you. The name was a joke about how thin she was, even though he was just as thin. As you look down at him you notice that he seems puffier now, like he's been slightly inflated. His neck is melting like wax over the collar of his shirt. The flesh looks soft and undulating, stuffed like an eclair. It seems to invite you to give it an exploratory poke. You squeeze your hands together to stop yourself from reaching out.

The day after his body was found your father came to his house to retrieve a suit for him to be buried in. It was your father who opened the laptop and found the letter, typed on Microsoft Word. He printed it out, brought it home to show your mother, and that night you slipped your hand into the inner pocket of his coat and retrieved it. The letter talked about the diagnosis, about how ashamed he was. It wasn't a disease you had ever heard of, and that night you looked it up on your father's computer. The three letters together, all caps, had seemed violent and frightening. The final line was, 'I'm so sorry.'

You spent the days before the funeral padding quietly around the house, trying not to fracture the glassy atmosphere. Your father had cried noisily – they'd been close – and your mother retreated, newly insubstantial, to her room, emerging only to make arrangements.

The door behind you creaks and a stranger's shadow appears beside yours on the beige wall. A stranger's hand lands on your shoulder and you look at the white hairs curling on the knuckles. A man's voice says, 'That's right, love, he's with God now,' and you realize it must have looked like you were praying.

Nine years old – April

Your pencil case is large and navy and rectangular and always has an apple in it for the mid-morning break. The bell will go in fifteen minutes. The round, ostentatious protrusion of the apple makes you feel uneasy. Your teacher, Miss Henner, is impossibly young and pretty, and when the class was reading *Matilda* you suggested they call her Miss Henney. She beamed at you, and you wanted to stay in the moment for ever.

You sit next to a girl named Ellen. She seems much older than the other girls. She's tall and her breasts have arrived. She wears a pink frilly training bra that shows through her thin school t-shirt. Her pencil case is always full of half-empty tubes of lip gloss and when the headmaster passes her in the hall she makes thrusting motions with her hips and rolls her tongue.

'Do you know what this is?'

You take your eyes off the apple outline and turn to her. She's holding something long and slim and wrapped in pale-yellow plastic. She waves it at you.

'Um.'

'Do you know what it does?'

You look at Miss Henner. She's leaning over a desk to help someone with a maths problem. Ellen laughs scornfully.

'You don't, do you? It's a tampon, stupid. Do you even know what a tampon's for?'

You do, in fact, although you've never seen one, and you're astonished that Ellen requires them already. You look at her pink frilly chest, and she leans over and taps your nose with the tampon. You flinch, and she laughs again.

'It won't bite!'

When the bell goes you stay in your seat. The classroom empties and you open your pencil case. You don't like apples, and you've spent every mid-morning break since the beginning of term trying to dispose of them discreetly around the school. For a while you tried to give them to other students, but one told a teacher who threatened to tell your mother if you didn't stop. You could imagine the discussion, her initial confusion that would soon give way to irritation. The thought of having to explain yourself pains you. Since then you've got rid of the apples by putting them in various bins around the school or hiding them in the hedges at the end of the playground. You take the apple and hold it in your hand for a moment, then look around. Hanging on the back of Ellen's chair is her school bag, which is huge and black and has faux-leather handles and isn't like a school bag at all. You drop the apple into its folds and depths, then go outside. The next day, you do the same again.

A week into your new ritual, the bell goes for lunchtime. Two boys jostle each other to see who can get out the door first. The taller one elbows the shorter one and he falls against Ellen's chair. She says, 'Watch it, idiot,' and shoves him away. The bag, hung on the edge of her chair, falls to the ground and six apples, all in various stages of decay, spill out on to the floor. It hadn't occurred to you that she wouldn't empty her bag at the end of each day. The oldest apple has been crushed under the weight of schoolbooks and PE plimsolls and a hairbrush and a slim, black flute case. It looks like a trodden-on homunculus. It bounces against your ankles, and when Ellen screams you scream too. The children closest to your desk gather round to look and when you join in the chorus of 'Ewww' it feels like someone else's voice in your mouth. Ellen shouts, 'What the hell?' and Miss Henner, who is ushering the others out of the classroom, says, 'Language, Ellen.' You are one of the last to leave, and when you are at the door you look back. Miss Henner is on her knees, gathering up the rotten apples. She watches you steadily from under her choppy, fashionable fringe.

Ten years old – October

You get 96 per cent in a practice entrance exam for one of the local secondary schools. Your teacher, a woman in her mid-forties called Mrs Doherty, sets the paper down on your desk and whispers, 'Well done, smarty-pants!' You say, 'The pants did most of the work,' and she laughs delightedly. Mrs Doherty wears long cardigans and has short, feathery hair the colour of burnt toast. As she goes through the answers with the rest of the class you are allowed to pass the time with an activity of your choice. You sit at the easel in the corner, painting lopsided cats using old, desiccated paintbrushes in varying sizes. On the first go you don't wait for the paint to dry on the paper before adding more and the colours weep into one another; a kitten's eyes seep black all over its yellow fur. You start again, and try to exercise patience.

As you wait by the school gates for your mother to pick you up, you inspect your painting again, pleased with this second draft. As the minutes pass, the other children are retrieved and led away and put into silver cars and black cars and red cars. Soon, you are the only one left. You hear Mrs Doherty call your name, and you turn and see her standing in the doorway, ensconced in her beige cardigan. She beckons you inside, explains that your mother isn't able to come, that your father will be picking you up, but he'll be a while.

When he appears in the classroom doorway you are back at the easel, this time painting tulips and sunflowers and daisies in a vase. He says, 'That's beautiful, love,' and when you get home he whispers, 'You can give it to your mum, soon as she's feeling better.' A pile of dirty laundry sits abandoned in front of the washing machine. You can hear the bath taps running upstairs.

Ten years old – May

The water, lit up silver-grey in parts, green-blue in others, glitters. It smells like salt and fish. It is one of those rare, untimely hot days, and you are at the coast. People are queueing for ice creams, the white, wet plumes the shape of helter-skelters. You are walking alongside your mother, licking melted chocolate off your fingers. She says, 'Look,' and gestures to the row of thick-legged men standing by the harbour edge, gripping fishing rods. As you approach them you can see the hooks drifting through the air. You imagine one of those hooks, fine as a syringe, edging its way behind your eye and snagging. You imagine your vision splitting as one eye stays on the dock and the other is tugged from your socket and borne across the sky, able to see the fluffy treetops and the boats and the featureless heads of pedestrians and the guilty fishing line, dividing the sky in two. You retreat, panicked. Keeping your eyes on the fishermen's movements, you fail to notice the stone bollard. You tumble backwards and sideways over it. Your temple smacks the concrete.

Moments later your mother is dabbing gently at the hot dribble of blood making its way towards your mouth. You feel dazed, and she makes you follow her finger with your eyes. You feel relief at not having unravelled like a ball of yarn. She says, 'Strange girl,' softly.

Eleven years old – September

'Want some?'

You are colouring in the margins of your exercise book with a biro. You turn. 'What?'

She shakes the packet of gum at you. 'Want a bit?'

You stare at her, and she laughs. 'Don't worry, I'm not saying your breath smells.'

You relax and take a piece. You always think the best part of chewing gum is the initial crack as you break the shell and feel the fragments disseminating through goo, like crushing the exoskeleton of some tiny creature between your teeth.

You hold the gum between your fingers and consider it. 'I heard that if you swallow gum it stays in your digestive system for seven years.'

She smiles, and you note that her smile doesn't go upward at either end, just gets wider and wider until it seems like her face might split in two. She says, 'That's a long time.'

'I know.'

'Well, I promise I won't make you swallow it.'

'Thank you.'

Her name is Rachael, and this is the longest conversation you have had since being seated next to each other alphabetically a fortnight ago. Secondary school is not how you imagined – everyone seems to have arrived with pre-assembled friendship groups, all at maximum capacity, and an awareness of their place in the social hierarchy. Nobody is actively unpleasant, but you've struggled to make friends, and you're grateful for the school's abundance of quiet corners. You contemplate Rachael's words, and choose your own carefully. 'If I did swallow it, could we have a party for it coming out the other side, seven years from now?'

She tilts her head at you. 'What, like a "Congratulations on your gummy poo" party?'

'Something like that.'

'Sure. What do you think we'll be doing in seven years?'

'Some very grown-up activity.'

'Like what?'

'Making pasta, maybe. Owning a house.'

'Maybe both.'

'A detached, two-bathroom home with a porch.'

'A drawer in the kitchen with one of those cutlery organizer things.'

'A load of condiments in the fridge.'

'A radiator key.'

'A carbon monoxide detector.'

'A first-aid kit.'

'A big green lawn.'

She pauses for a second. 'A green – sorry, did you just say *lorn*? Like, L-O-R-N?'

You frown and say slowly, 'No, lawn.'

She laughs. 'Oh, sorry.'

'Why would I have said lorn?'

'I don't know.'

'What's a lorn?'

'I don't know.'

'Am I a lorn?'

'Shut up.'

'Sorry, am I making you feel a bit' – you pause – 'forlorn?'

'Shut *up*.'

'Is this your first time visiting Earth?'

'Apparently.'

'Let me introduce you to our ways and customs.'

'Yes – teach me all about your lorns.'

The teacher, a too-tall man with Playmobil hair, looks up and says, 'Girls,' in a warning voice. Rachael sniggers breathily. You take this moment to put the gum in your mouth and bite down. When he has turned his attention back to his computer she resumes whispering. 'So, seven years from now we'll cook some pasta and eat it on the lorn and you can poo out your gum and we'll have a party. Sound good?'

You swallow, feeling the ball of gum edge its way down your throat. You think about how furious your mother would be if she could see you doing this – how vigilant she is about choking hazards. Rachael pats you on the arm in solidarity. You smile, and the unprecedented force of it makes you aware of your cheeks.

'Sounds good,' you say.

Eleven years old – December

Every Christmas you give your father the same gift: a black plastic wallet from the Debenhams men's department. Every year you sit next to the tree and watch him open it. Every year he expresses loud pleasure. 'Great! This one was just about done – thanks, pet!' Then he'll slide the wallet from the previous year out of the pocket of his jeans. He'll transfer his credit cards and his driving licence with the picture where he has more hair and his loyalty card for the sandwich bar and his membership card for one of the local teams' supporters' club and a handful of old receipts.

This year you stand for a long time in the men's section, gripping the ten-pound note and the five-pound note your mother gave you. She loiters near by, idly fingering leather gloves. There is a sale on, and the plastic wallets are reduced to £6.50. You slide four brown wallets off the silver hook to retrieve a black one, and then you wander through the shop, inspecting ties and socks and cufflinks shaped like footballs with silver hexagons and red hexagons. You find a flipbook 'Word a Day' calendar, and flick through it. 'Barbarism'. 'Fenestration'. 'Moribund'. It costs £9.99, and your mother gives you the additional pound coins.

When your father opens the present and finds the calendar he is surprised. He starts to thumb through the plastic sheets, sounding words out to you like a child. *Aw-spish-ee-us*. He smiles and says jokily, 'You trying to say something about my vocabulary?' and you are aghast at the suggestion. He laughs, pushes his lips down on your scalp. He gets to work rehoming his loyalty card.

Eleven years old – February 11th

'Is that a new hairband?'
　'What?'
　'Your hairband, is it new?'

'No.'

'Oh. Have you had your hair cut?'

'No.'

Charlie's scrutiny unsettles you. She smiles at you and reveals the gap between her two front teeth. Her blonde hair hangs densely over one shoulder. You imagine how thick and soft it must feel, and you want to wrap your hands up in it. Your stomach yodels with hunger – today is the anniversary of your uncle's death and, as has become tradition, your mother's bedroom door remained closed this morning as you dressed haphazardly for school, choosing an additional half-hour in bed over breakfast. The lunch queue shuffles slowly towards the hatch and you will it faster. You look at Rachael; Charlie and Bethany are her friends, not yours. She looks at you, then at Charlie, confused, and you take comfort from knowing it's not just you who doesn't understand. Charlie persists.

'But you've done something to your hair though, right?'

'No, it's just normal.'

She laughs, and it's like crockery breaking. 'Look, just touch your hair, OK?'

'What?'

'Put your hand up and touch your hair.'

'Why?'

'I want to show Beth something.'

'Um.'

You raise your right hand. You turn your head to look as well, curious. You have PE after lunch, and you are already dressed in your sports shirt with the capped sleeves, ready to swing a tennis racket. You realize, too late, what is happening. Bethany looks at your armpit and giggles, and you see, as though for the first time, the wispy brown hairs. Her giggle persists, and you want to grip her big cheeks in your hands and smash her head against the window. You feel a greater animosity towards her than Charlie, even, because of the sheer arbitrariness of her position as Charlie's favoured acolyte. You clamp your arm to your side and look away. Charlie laughs again.

'So, I guess you just don't shave anywhere, do you?' and she looks towards your blue shorts. 'Lucky boys,' she says and upturns her mouth in exaggerated distaste. She laughs some more.

It's true, you don't shave, and it hadn't occurred to you that you ought to. You look at the matching hairs on your shins and knees. You look at Rachael, helpless. Her face has gone red, but when you look down at her legs you notice for the first time that the skin is like Barbie-doll plastic. You wonder how she'd known when to start doing these things, and why she hadn't told you. Charlie turns away from you and picks up a tray. She doesn't address you for the remainder of lunch.

'Mum?'

'What is it?'

'Will you get me some razors?'

She sighs. 'What?'

'Will you get me some razors, please?'

'What for?'

'So I can shave my legs.'

She angles her laptop away from you and turns in her seat.

'Why on earth would you want to start shaving your legs?'

'They're hairy.'

'You're eleven years old. That's far too young to start with that nonsense. Don't be so silly.'

'Girls at school are doing it.'

'Well, they're silly as well. The hair on your legs is fine and soft and basically invisible. Once you start shaving it'll grow back thicker and it'll become something you have to do all the time. Your leg hair is perfectly acceptable.'

You pause, and she raises her eyebrows at you.

'What about my armpits?'

'Wait until you actually need to start shaving, OK?'

'OK.'

'Have you done your maths for tomorrow?'

'Yes.' You haven't.

'Well, I'm busy, so can you give me some peace?'

'Yeah.' You turn, then turn back. 'What if I just borrowed one of your razors?'

Her knuckles are white as she grips the table edge. 'I am going to scream.'

'OK, OK.'

'Go and do something useful.'

'OK.'

'Yes?'

You pause. 'OK.' She glares at you, and turns back to her laptop. You do a loop of the kitchen before leaving, and twist your head to read what's on the screen. I'M THE PROOF YOU CAN LIVE HAPPILY WITH HIV, the headline says. Below the words is a photograph of a man, smiling. You leave the room.

Twelve years old – August

You are sitting midway up the staircase, clutching your knees and breathing lightly. You have a magic trick: you stand on the bottom stair and march on the spot, making your footsteps lighter with each two-four stroke so it sounds like you are going upstairs. Once that's done, you sit and listen to your parents talking behind the closed kitchen door. You wonder if they listen out for your going upstairs, if your efforts are appreciated.

'You never listen to me. You never support me.'

Your mother is like a horror-film scarecrow when she's angry; her bony hands crackle at her sides, her voice stays low and threatening, yellow cotton wisps of her hair come loose from the little lump of bun. Often the small, round detachedness of her bun reminds you of the neat scrotum on the neighbours' blond Labrador.

'Th-th-that's rich, coming from you.'

Your father becomes instantly flustered at confrontation. His face turns dark red and he stutters, like he's finding his tongue in his mouth for the first time. There is a pause.

'What on earth do you mean by that?'

Your mother can make any word poisonous. *Earth*.

'When I wrote that feature for the club's newsletter you didn't say anything! You didn't even read it. So it's not like you support me either.'

You grip your legs tighter and hold your breath. There had been a change in management at the local football club; the general consensus was that the change was negative. Your father had done some research into the club's history, charting the highs and lows of the team's performance, drawing correlations between management style and financial backing and league success. He had written a 1,000-word article, which had been published. There is another, longer, pause.

'That was two, fucking, years ago.'

The expletive surprises you – your mother rarely swears, instead she makes normal words as dangerous as 'fuck' or 'shit'. There is a long silence and you can imagine your father's useless mouth, gaping. When his helpless reply comes – 'You know, you'd think with everything that's happened, with what happened to your brother, you might have a little perspective' – you know that he has lost, that he won't be permitted to say anything more. You don't stay for your mother's closing remarks, satisfied that you will not be a topic of conversation tonight. You wander upstairs, not bothering to hide your footsteps.

Thirteen years old – May

The tacky white clock on the assembly wall clunks like a tongue. You grip your pen and force yourself to look at the page in front of you. You are forty-five minutes into your English Lit exam. You want desperately to do well in it – you are terrified that you are becoming slow and stupid, and you are worried that the teachers in the English department don't like you, or worse, don't think about you at all. Your marks have gone down this year and you have given up speaking in class. This exam is on a book called *The War*

Orphan. You have not enjoyed it, nor had you enjoyed the novel the year before, *Goodnight Mister Tom*.

You wish your class could read books about something other than war and the children of war; you want to read about normal people trying to do normal things. You want to know in detail what the characters look like, what they are wearing in each scene, what they think about when they look at themselves in the mirror, what happens when they try to walk quickly when the ground is frozen and slippery, what they say when they get an unexpected phone call. You suspect the horrors of war are easier to navigate emotionally – everything is awful and so there is only one way to respond to it, with hopelessness, sadness. Normal life seems more difficult, and you want instructions on how to move through the world.

You are struggling to remember a lengthy quote about loneliness when you feel an unfamiliar pain in your abdomen, like some previously dormant animal inside you is stretching. It is 3:20 p.m., not even halfway through the two-hour exam. You leave a two-line gap on the page for the quote, try to continue writing, but minute by minute the pain gets worse, and like a lighthouse beam it flashes, then fades. By 3:40 p.m. it is all-consuming, and when the beam is at its brightest your whole body constricts. A girl at the next desk, a classmate whose name you can't currently remember – although you have seen the naked photo of her that was promulgated throughout the school – glances over. The alarm on her face frightens you. You raise a hand that feels fizzy and heavy, hot and cold, and a teacher whispers that you are excused. The last word you have written is 'indiccative' and you think, as you walk to the bathroom, about how disappointed your mother would be at your spelling it wrong.

You sit on the toilet with your head against the wall of the stall, clammy and amazed by the red Rorschach test on your pants and upper thighs. You are crying, softly. The bathroom door opens and you hear the high-heeled footsteps of an English teacher, a tall and upright woman who wears pastel cardigans with mismatching buttons. She asks if you are OK and when you say, with a wet, undignified gulp, 'I think I got my period,' her soft 'Oh' response makes you wonder if you should have said something else. You hear the metallic *thunk* of the machine on the wall. She slides three green squares under the door.

After the exam has ended you go outside and wait for the bus. You wonder if people can tell by looking at you that there has been a messy and public bloodletting. Rachael rushes over, and you tell her what happened. She rubs your back and says, 'You poor thing,' before turning to tell Charlie, who has arrived unnoticed. Her hair has been recently made blonder, and her whole head seems luminous. She smiles, at first kindly, but then it becomes something else, and she says loudly, 'I really don't think that's normal, you know. Are you sure there isn't something wrong with you?' She gestures at your crotch. 'Down there?' You say nothing.

Rachael and Charlie and Bethany are walking into town. Rachael asks if you want to come but before you can respond Charlie says, 'You probably want to go home and get sorted out.' She pulls the others away and calls back in a sing-song voice, 'Hope you feel better,' and it occurs to you, too late, that this day has marked you out, again, as wrong, and strange, and different.

Fourteen years old – October

'I got you this! He's cute, right?'

Your father has returned from a conference in Wales. He presents you with your gift: a red, squashy dragon. It has black-bead eyes and a toothy smile. Your mother frowns at it and says, 'Isn't she a bit old for that?' over the top of your head. Your father looks wounded and you shake your head with conviction. You press the dragon tight to your chest. Your mother opens her gift. It's a scarf; heavy brocade. It looks expensive and comes sheathed in dark-green tissue paper. Your mother never wears scarves, and you press your thumbs into the dragon's fat belly and watch her nervously. She says, 'Thank you,' and it sounds as though it was whispered under water.

A week after his return you sit up in bed, listening to them argue. Your father says, 'But I just got you that scarf!' And when your mother replies it is so quietly that you have to lean forward to hear. 'All that scarf tells me is that my husband doesn't look at me any more,' and then, louder, 'That scarf is an overpriced reminder that we don't know each other.' You grip your dragon – in the dark it's just another blur.

Fifteen years old – September

'What are you doing this weekend?'

'I'm not sure.'

'Want to go to the park?'

'What's in the park?'

'Trees, grass, swings, maybe a dog or two.'

'What's trees?'

Rachael smiles. You are sitting in class, waiting for the teacher to arrive. She plays the game.

'Ah, trees are the big green-headed people.'

'Ohhh, the cauliflower men.'

'Yes.'

'And dogs?'

'Dogs are trickier.'

'The small, wet-nosed horse men.'

'You are learning so much about our world.'

'I hope to hear the song of the hand-sized music men.'

'You mean the birds?'

'Ah, yes. *Bir*-irds.'

'You know so much of space travel and yet you are so like a child in some ways.'

'On my planet the rich crop season brings much plenty.'

'Perhaps you might share your bounty with us.'

You shrug. 'Maybe. I'll see how I feel, lorn.'

She shakes with laughter and throws her head back, like in a television car crash. You smile at her, and your head feels light. She elbows you lightly.

'So, weirdo, the park?'

'OK. Will it just be us?'

'Of course. It's going to be beautiful and restorative and I'll have you all to myself.'

You smile again and say, 'OK,' and she puts her arm around your shoulders.

'What's going on?'

Charlie is laughing into the back of her hand: a wet, noiseless snigger. She's wearing low, tight jeans and a short, yellow t-shirt, and you can't stop staring at the shadows and lumps of her abdominal muscles. When she has stopped making that forced, wet-grass squeak of a laugh she leans back and raises her eyebrows at you.

'Do you know what a snow blow is?'

You made your father stop washing his car – a red Honda – to drive you to the park. Halfway there you got a text from Rachael saying, **Dont bother coming.** You asked your father to take you home. He said, 'You sure, sweetie?' And you nodded and he did a three-point turn in someone's drive-way. Five minutes later you got another text. **Sorry. Charlie stole my phone. Come!** This time your father had to make a U-turn in the road. He swore loudly, gave the finger to a cyclist in a reflective jacket. The unrinsed droplets of soap flew off the windows and windscreen of the car.

You look down at your trainers, at the individual streaks of grass stuck around the white rubber soles. You speak quietly. 'Um, no.'

'Have you ever given someone a blowjob?'

'No.'

'Do you even know what a blowjob is?'

'Yes, of course.' Rachael had told you.

'Have you ever kissed anyone?'

'Yes.'

'Who?'

'There was a guy I met on holiday once.'

The lie is so obvious it doesn't bear acknowledgement. She smiles.

'Has anyone ever told you that you look a bit like one of the dogs from the Hush Puppies ad? You know, the really sad-looking ones with the big floppy ears?' She turns to Rachael and Bethany. 'Doesn't she?' Bethany laughs uncertainly. Rachael looks at you, apologetic. The ground feels damp under the seat of your trousers.

'So, who do you fancy?'

'I don't know.'

'Come on. Who would you like to give a blowjob to?'

'I don't – I haven't thought about it.'

'What about,' and she scratches idly at one of the iron curves on her stomach, 'Michael Jamison?'

Michael Jamison is beautiful and three years ahead of you at school. He is a mythic figure, only ever spoken about with piety, using both his first and last name.

You shrug. 'Yeah, sure, I guess.'

Rachael told you once that Charlie does five hundred sit-ups a day, that she only eats carrots dipped in hummus for dinner, that she lost her virginity at fourteen to a guy she didn't know, pressed up against a wall outside a club.

She smiles at you. You think you could slide a pair of closed tweezers into the gap between her teeth and then let them spring open, each tooth pushed further to either side, or perhaps coming loose from the gum completely. She leans forward.

'You know he's gay, right? I heard he has HIV, even, which is basically AIDS. You want to fuck a gay guy with AIDS?'

'No, I – you said—'

'I could totally imagine you fucking a fag.'

'I didn't say that.'

'You can't take it back.'

Bethany pulls her phone out of her backpack and starts tapping at it. Her opal-coloured rosary beads peek out through the open zip. She carries them everywhere, even to school. Charlie has demanded Bethany get her a black set to wear on nights out, even though Charlie isn't the right religion for rosary beads. You stare at Bethany until she looks up. She gives you a nervous smile. You don't understand how Bethany has been deemed normal, when her public celebrating of religion and her rosary beads and her refusal to swear are all reasons for her to be labelled strange, and yet you, whose strangeness is mostly invisible, are the one Charlie turns her attention to. You continue to stare at Bethany, try to detect a heightened level of spirituality from her, but she looks away. If you were braver you would ask, 'And how does God feel about snow blows and fucking and cruelty?' The sun sits on the surface of the treetops like an ornament, and you hold your hand to your eyebrows to stop yourself from looking at it. You can feel a hot prickling behind your eyes, a thickness in your throat.

'Jesus, don't cry.'

An elderly couple is walking close to the trees, holding hands. She's wearing a red padded body warmer with a striped black and red fleece underneath. Her hand is gripped in his. You wish you were her.

'I don't want—' and you stop because you can hear the bubbles rising up into your words.

'If you don't want to fuck Michael Jamison you have to do something.' At this Rachael and Bethany look up: Bethany curious, Rachael anxious.

'What?'

'You have to pull your trousers down.'

'What?'

'Pull your trousers down and count to sixty and then you can pull them back up.'

'Here?'

'Yep. So we can all see. Who knows, maybe you'll give that old guy a hard-on.'

Rachael says uncertainly, 'Charlie,' but Charlie keeps her eyes fixed on you. She runs her tongue over her front teeth.

'Go. Do it.'

'I don't want to.'

'If you don't then I'm going to tell everyone you want to fuck Michael Jamison, and then everyone will know you're going to get AIDS. Nobody will want to talk to you.'

When you stand up from the grass you avoid eye contact. You put your hands to your back – the bottom of your t-shirt is slightly wet. You walk towards the edge of the green, to where the barbed-wire fence signals the beginning of the public allotments. You hear Charlie say, 'Can't wait to see those hairy knees.' You can see the smudged glass of the greenhouses, the four shovels propped up against a wooden crate. When you bend over you can make out the small, brown outline of a rabbit, making its way across the soil. Long-eared soft man, you think. The early-evening air is cold around the tops of your thighs; you look down and imagine you can see it looping pale blue between your legs. You look up and try to find the rabbit, but it's gone. You count the green protrusions of new vegetables in the ground but lose count after twenty-three. You find the other thirty-seven seconds in the diamond-shaped gaps in the fence.

You pull your trousers up. You turn and see Charlie and Bethany at the far end of the green, their backs to you, the soles of their canvas trainers appearing and disappearing as they kick their legs behind them and get gradually smaller. Soon, they're gone. Rachael remains on the grass, her arms around her legs and her expression unreadable. She gives you a small wave, and you already know you'll forgive her. Rachael has been granted the gift of inoffensiveness; she invites neither scrutiny nor ridicule, and how could you ask her to jeopardize that, to protect you? As you make your way back across the park you look around and realize the elderly couple has disappeared. You wonder if they were in on the joke too.

Fifteen years old – January

You and Rachael are in the school toilets, bouncing a small rubber ball back and forth. The door opens and a Russian girl named Nastja walks in. She stands by the sinks, watching you. She has only recently arrived at the school, and she wears white woollen tights with her school skirt and speaks in broken English. You and Rachael continue to bounce the ball. Rachael continues to talk about her breasts.

'I thought going on the pill would make them grow, but it just made my ass and hips fatter.'

'Did it?' You crane your neck.

'Yes, it did, and stop staring at my ass.'

'Maybe they could take your ass and put it on your chest.' She laughs. 'That'd be nice.'

'They're not that small, though, are they?'

'Maybe compared to yours, or the first years', but I went for a run yesterday and realized half a mile in that I'd forgotten to put on a sports bra. That does not bode well.'

You bounce the ball back to her and she tries to hold it in place underneath her cleavage. It drops to the floor. 'See?' she says. The ball rolls away and stops at Nastja's foot. She looks down at it, then back up at you.

'Hey, Nastja,' Rachael says, 'you all right? Want to play?'

Nastja nods uncertainly, picks up the ball. She throws it at the ground and it careens off the tiles then hits the ceiling then bounces off the walls. It smacks the window behind you and you catch it.

Rachael laughs. 'Yeah, it can go a bit mad if you bounce too hard.'

Nastja nods, and giggles. Her laugh is high-pitched, like bells. You look at her and wonder if boys think she's sexy. She has big brown eyes and shoulder-length, lustrous, dark hair. Her skin is smooth and her lips are full. You suspect that if boys don't think she's sexy it's only because of the white tights and the broken English. You suspect that anywhere else, dressed in anything else, she would be considered beautiful.

The three of you bounce the ball for a while. Occasionally other girls come in to use the toilets and you all pause, eye them with soft hostility, resume when they leave. Eventually Rachael says, 'Shit, I was supposed to go talk to Mrs Burke about that internship. Here' – and she bounces the ball to you – 'you guys keep playing. I'll see you in class. Bye, Nastja.' She smiles and leaves. Now that it is just you and the Russian, you worry about the moment's equilibrium. You bounce the ball to her and she catches it, then returns it. You carry on in silence for a few moments.

'Do you like it here?'

She looks startled, and you wonder if your voice sounds strange when people hear it addressed to them, for the first time. She shrugs.

'It is OK. The classrooms are very cold.'

She's right. The school's central heating system is unreliable and clunky. 'Is that why' – you gesture at her legs – 'the tights?'

She looks down. 'I'm sorry?'

'The tights, is that why you wear them? They're warm?'

She looks back at you, and speaks slowly. 'Yes. They keep me quite warm.'

'That's good.'

You bounce the ball to her, and she holds it in her hands. She has elegant fingers, with two gold rings on her right-hand index.

'Rachael is your friend?'

'Yeah.'

'Your best friend?'

You stare at her. She looks back, placidly.

'Um. Yes.'

She bounces the ball to you, and says dreamily, 'It's good

to have friends.' You look at her legs in their white tights and notice for the first time that they're shapely, that her shins curve gently outwards and her thighs are slim. You notice how slender her neck is, emerging from the baggy grey jumper. You spy the spheres of her breasts, noticeable underneath it. You wonder what you must look like to her, large and shapeless. You say, 'Yeah, it is,' and bounce the ball too hard. It hits the floor, ricochets sideways off the wall and disappears into a stall. You hear a plop. Nastja says, 'Oh!' and while thinking about the ball in the toilet you also think that that 'Oh!' could be used in an ad for French perfume or some expensive almond liqueur. You both wander towards the stall, and peer in. The ball is bobbing on the surface of the water. You turn to Nastja. 'Can you get it?'

'What?' Her eyes go bigger.

'The ball. Can you reach in and grab it?'

She smiles uncertainly, and you notice how evenly spaced her teeth are. She laughs that bell-laugh again. You gesture at the toilet.

'Seriously, can you get it for me? It's Rachael's ball. She'll be upset that we lost it.'

'I—' Nastja starts, and then she pauses. She looks at you, worried.

'I won't tell anyone,' you say quickly. 'Just reach in and grab it. Go on. Do it now, before it disappears.'

Nastja uses her other hand, the one not wearing the gold rings. She pulls up her jumper sleeve and you notice she has a small tattoo of a sunflower on her inner wrist. When she tries to grab the ball it sinks deeper and she has to reach in further. When she brings her hand out water is trickling off her forearm. She holds it out to you.

'Here,' she says.

The ball has a marble pattern in dark green and dark blue. You won it from a machine at the bowling alley. You look up at Nastja.

'It looks like fruit, doesn't it?' you say.

'Um. Yes, I suppose,' she says, and she reaches it towards you.

'You could take a bite out of it,' you say, and once more there's that uncertain bell-laugh. The ball has a wet sheen to it now. Fluid drips off it on to the tiles. You look at Nastja and shape your face into a grimace.

'It's all pissy and disgusting,' you say. 'You should just get rid of it.' You turn and walk out of the bathroom. The bell rings.

Sixteen years old – June

The night before your GCSE history exam, two days after your sixteenth birthday, you sit with your textbook open on your thighs, open at the section on Kristallnacht. You are texting a boy from your year: Scott. He's tall and has an extreme overbite, and a few weeks ago in the library he invited you to poke his erection through the fabric of his trousers. You did, and giggled.

Outside you can hear the music of an ice-cream van and you tell him you are listening to 'Ring a Ring o' Roses'.

He replies quickly, asking if you know it's a plague song. You say yes, even though you didn't. He replies again, asking if you know an asteroid is on course to hit the Earth in twelve years, that you will die at the age of twenty-eight.

You both take fencing on Tuesday afternoons, a private-school affectation introduced by the school's largely absent headmaster. It has now become the sport option for people who aren't good at team sports or who have blood disorders. Rachael, Bethany and Charlie all take hockey. You chose fencing because you knew Scott was doing it, and because you get to sit on a bench for an hour and not do anything. The coach is a man called Big Fred. He's from New Zealand and he smells like dog shit. He always insists on helping you into the heavy, starched fencing jacket that reeks of old sweat. Scott often jokes that Big Fred wants to sleep with you, and you like that the joke centres on the idea that you could be desirable.

After he tells you about the asteroid you struggle to concentrate on studying. When he texts you again, a series of question marks, you still don't reply. You try to imagine yourself at twenty-eight. You picture the woman from the Nice'n Easy semi-permanent hair colour ad. You imagine that you're her, that you have glossy chestnut hair and a shoulder bag and a beige blazer. It's a sunny day and the light bounces off you. A disembodied voice in the sky says, 'Nice'n Easy! The hair colour that doesn't look like hair colour!'

You try to imagine dying by asteroid. There will be a low boom, a slight rustle in the ends of your hair. The air will thicken with dust, and sand will settle on your sleeves.

Glass windows in shopfronts and synagogues will burst out of their frames. You will turn, and a wall of black will rush towards you, and then: nothing. You are nothing. Everything is nothing. You realize you won't even have the capacity to think 'I'm nothing'. You won't have the ability to register you're no longer existing. There will only be oblivion. You try, for a few moments, to not think anything. You start to panic.

Sixteen years old – November

'How was the party?'

Rachael shrugs. 'Pretty dull. You should have come.'

'I wasn't invited.'

'Like that's any kind of reason.'

'What did you wear?'

'Black jeans and a top.'

'What kind of top?'

'Low cut, sparkly.'

'Did you wear a bra under it?'

'A strapless one.'

'Could you see it?'

'Probably.'

'What did Charlie wear?'

'Just come next time, weirdo. It'll save me having to relay all the minutiae after.'

'What did you drink?'

Rachael sighs. 'Rum and coke.'

'Did you get drunk?'

'A little.'

'What's it like?'

'Sort of warm and wet and blurry.'

'Was it scary?'

'Not at all. In fact, I think you'd really enjoy it. You could be less thinky.'

You consider this for a moment. Rachael looks at you and laughs. 'Exactly.'

'What did Charlie wear?'

'You are bloody relentless.'

'Well?'

She sighs. 'A gold dress. Tight, short. You know what she's like.'

You don't really know what she's like.

'She brought a girl with her, though.'

'A girl?'

'Yeah. I think they're dating.'

'Charlie's gay?'

'Yeah. I mean, she hasn't said it in as many words, but I think this was her wonderfully dramatic way of telling us, by draping herself over a tattoo artist all night.'

'What does she look like?'

'Short, dark hair. Tattoos, unsurprisingly. Very pretty, because she'd have to be.'

You pause, and think.

'So, Charlie's a fag, but she probably won't get AIDS.'

Rachael turns and looks at you. Her lips turn downwards. She waits a moment before speaking.

'That's a really fucking weird thing to say. Jesus Christ, don't fucking say shit like that.'

She walks on, and you realize she doesn't remember. At

least not as vividly as you. You stop, frozen with indignity. She turns back. It's starting to rain.

'You coming, weirdo?'

You don't say anything. She sighs and walks towards you. She makes an exasperated gesture with her hands.

'There was a dog at the party.'

You pause. 'Yeah?'

'Yeah. A wet-nosed, small, brown horse man.'

She smiles, and she pokes you until you smile back.

'C'mon, weirdo.'

You resume the walk into town. She links arms to show you that you are forgiven. You wish she knew that, in this instance, for once, it wasn't you who required forgiveness.

Sixteen years old – January

The anthropomorphized vulva smiles at you from your web browser in various shades of pink and red. White arrows move across it, showing you how to navigate yourself. Your new year's resolution is to be normal, to be knowing, to be sexual. The vulva has promised you the keys to the kingdom of adult pleasure. You hold a compact mirror between your open legs and immediately take it away when you see the vermilion skin, the colour of a squalling newborn's face, and the brown hairs scattered across it. You keep your eyes fixedly on the drawing's encouraging expression and put your fingers between your 45-degree-splayed thighs. The skin is dry and uncompromising, and when you wodge your fingers in, it feels like something that shouldn't be there, like a popcorn kernel between two teeth. You slide them out and move them around the periphery. You try to identify all the different attachments of your anatomy. The vulva references your 'clitoral hood' and you cringe. You venture inside again, press further this time, allow your finger to stir your insides, and wait. When the disquietude begins to encroach – why aren't you feeling anything? – you give up. The vulva's once-encouraging smile now seems condemnatory. You close the laptop.

Seventeen years old – September

'This is a rather disparate selection.'

The careers tutor, Mr Hughes, is an angular man in his sixties. On his desk is a framed photograph of him and his wife. His wife is short and round and has a grey bob and a green pashmina. She fits into the space under his arm. When you look at the photograph you find yourself feeling jealous of her, of their lives together, of their grown-up, moved-away children and their grey hair and their annual holidays to Italy or Spain or Portugal. It seems neat and scripted and preordained and you want all of it.

Mr Hughes has a salt-and-pepper moustache that conceals his upper lip entirely. When he speaks his mouth resembles a long, tufty caterpillar walking on a treadmill. You find it difficult to listen to him, so distracting is the gentle vibration of the thick hairs. He chews on every syllable.

'I get the impression you may not have given this much thought.'

You like Mr Hughes a lot. You like the mauve skin of his eyelids and the wiry hairs on the backs of his hands and wrists. You like that he seems to operate within one register, that you are of so little consequence to him that nothing you could do would anger or upset him. The slow, deep rumble of his voice calms you. In this case, however, Mr Hughes is wrong: the problem is that you have given the assignment – to compile a list of prospective university courses – entirely too much thought. As a result law, social work, history, travel & tourism, film studies, politics, nursing and occupational therapy are just some of the options you have written down.

'I felt it might be silly to fence myself in too much.'

You look around the room, and then down at your lap, confronted for the first time with your temporality. You wonder how you have wound up here, in this position, already. Your grades never improved as you thought they would, and at some point you stopped being the person who could make a teacher laugh, who was allowed to crochet with coloured wool while the other students went through solutions to maths problems you had already solved. At some point you became someone teachers didn't think of as special and clever. You look at Mr Hughes, urging him to tell you otherwise. He looks like he might be suppressing a smile.

'On the contrary, my dear, you strike me as someone who might benefit from some fencing.'

Seventeen years old – November

Rachael inspects her plastic spoon. 'It's not even, like, objectively good ice cream.'

'I know.'

'Like, if you were to take a mouthful of some fancy-ass gelato from Italy, and then take a mouthful of this, it would probably just taste thin and flimsy and shit.'

You look into the cup. 'It's just cold wet.'

'That's it, exactly. That's all this is: cold wet.'

'And yet.'

'And yet I love it so much, if you told me I could never have it again I would threaten to throw your firstborn into a volcano.'

'That should be their slogan.'

'I reckon in a few years they'll realize they don't even have to try to entice us with a slogan.'

'McDonald's: you're going to eat it anyway.'

'McDonald's: like we could stop you.'

The rain berates the windscreen of your mother's black Toyota, your newly acquired R plate peeling at the corners. The car park is quiet – it's 10 p.m. and the surrounding furniture shops and DIY and gardening megastores are closed. The light from the yellow arches sets fire to the water droplets on the wing mirrors. You and Rachael pass a paper sack of wilting chips back and forth and eat them between mouthfuls of cold, wet ice cream. When the bag and cups are empty Rachael reclines her seat and closes her eyes.

You turn the key in the ignition. 'Shall we go?'

'Let's ride, cowgirl.'

You put the car into first, ease your foot off the clutch, press down on the accelerator. Nothing happens. You press down a little harder, the engine growls, the car stays still. You put all your weight on your right foot and the car strains forward, but with difficulty. Keeping your foot pressed down you heave across the car park, the engine groaning. It feels like something is pulling on the car from behind, and you look back over your shoulder, just to be sure.

Rachael opens her eyes. 'What's going on?'

'I don't know.'

The rain gets heavier and you put the wipers to the most extreme setting. They flurry across the windscreen, repelling the water in arcs. You look down at your feet. The Toyota continues its snail-speed progression, its mechanisms humming.

'Shit,' Rachael says suddenly. 'Is the handbrake on?'

'Oh,' you say. 'Whoops.'

You push it down and the car finally stops protesting. It glides across the tarmac. You put the brake on and look at Rachael. You bare your bottom teeth, sheepish.

'Ladies and gentlemen' – she laughs – 'may I present your woman motorist of the year.'

'Whoops,' you say again.

'You know what all this excitement has put me in the mood for?'

'Another ice cream?'

'You know it.'

You turn the steering wheel and swoop back towards the drive-through.

'McDonald's,' you say, 'because living is hard.'

'McDonald's,' she says, 'because how the fuck are you going to cope in the real world?'

Seventeen years old – December

The girl at the front of the hall is wearing a short tartan skirt and a black turtleneck and black tights and black brogues. She has long straight hair. You think she's beautiful.

'And live from the assembly hall, it's *Clueless*, the musical.'

You turn at the sound of Charlie's voice. She slides in next to Bethany, who is sitting next to Rachael, who is sitting next to you. Bethany laughs but says nothing, and you wonder if she's happy. She has long since stopped bringing her rosary beads to school or social events, and you realize you can't remember the last time you heard her speak. You wonder if she likes her life, or if she, like you, is dependent on the idea that things will improve.

'Ex-pupil,' Rachael says. 'I think she goes to uni in Bath. Or Exeter. Newcastle? I don't know. Somewhere English, somewhere posh.'

'Well, that explains the shoes,' Charlie says, and now you wonder if Charlie could explain the jokes she makes, if asked.

The girl is twenty-two, a final-year student. She did one year of Linguistics before switching to Literature. She makes a joke about being a year older than her course mates, feeling geriatric. The way she smiles lets you know she doesn't actually feel bad about it, and seems to give you permission to laugh. She talks about how she wasn't especially happy at school, that she struggled to feel comfortable, or passionate, but that going to university changed that. You wonder if the teachers standing at the side of the hall feel attacked by this, if they feel like they failed in their duty of care. If she is worried about offending them she doesn't show it, and you think you would like to go to the cinema with her, that it would be nice to sit in the dark next to this girl and be made to feel comfortable by her obvious comfort, but without having to say anything.

Every so often you hear Charlie mutter something; at one point it's 'I'm a dyke and not even I would wear that jumper', and you wonder if she feels eclipsed by this older, meadowy girl who has found a joy that exists far away and regardless of any of you. She finishes her talk by saying, 'Just remember, if *I* can do it,' and she crosses her eyes for a second, 'any of you can!' And you are all invited to laugh again at her warm self-deprecation.

As you file out of the hall Rachael starts talking about the plans for her eighteenth birthday. The four of you will take a train to the coast and stay overnight in a youth hostel that has a nightclub popular with underage students. When Charlie speaks it is only by the tone of her voice that you know she is addressing you – she smirks down at her hands and picks at one of her silver fingernails.

'Are you sure you're able to come? Not that we don't want you, it's just you shouldn't feel bad if you have something else on.'

Rachael says, 'She's just joking,' and Charlie says, 'Obviously.' You look over your shoulder at the girl in the turtleneck, who is laughing with one of the English teachers. You notice how her legs aren't especially thin, but that it hasn't stopped her wearing a short skirt. You notice that it hasn't stopped her from being beautiful. You want to be her. You give Charlie an enormous smile. She frowns. You affect an Australian accent.

'Course I'm comin', you daftie.'

She recoils. 'God, you're so fucking weird.'

You laugh, and your steps feel light. That evening you spend hours looking at prospectuses online.

Seventeen years old – January

'I notice you have Law at Northampton as one of your choices.'

'I like that they give you a year working at a firm once you finish your degree.'

You smile at Mr Hughes, knowledgeable, but not smug. You have done your research now, and you are certain that everything will be fine. He closes his eyes for a minute and you stare at the crushed velvet of his closed lids. When he opens them his eyes are remorseful and his lower lip slides from side to side under his moustache.

'Unfortunately, you are not the only astute student to notice that about the Northampton course.'

'Um, OK.'

'By which I mean it is very difficult to get a place.'

On the desk in front of him is a prospectus for a low-grade university, the sort you hear other students joking about when they're worrying about exams: *At this rate I'll end up at* _____*!* On the open page is a photo of a boy with unfashionable, thin-framed grey glasses and a lazy eye. His smile is goofy, his teeth pale yellow. You don't want to go to a university where this boy is deemed a good representative. You won't find your tartan-skirt, long-hair happiness at a place like that. You smile hopefully across the desk at Mr Hughes. Your voice is plaintive.

'Yeah, but I've figured out that if I work really hard this term and if my January results are OK then I can meet the grade requirements.'

Mr Hughes pauses. You wonder, absently, if you might start crying.

'Again, my dear, unfortunately, as is the case with many things in life' – and here he slides his clasped hands on the table so that they are sitting next to your hands, which are balled into two snail-shell-shaped fists – 'meeting the minimum requirements is rarely all that is needed of us.'

Your voice squeaks like a hinge. 'Oh. OK.'

'And . . .' and here he takes the longest pause. You lose the rhythm of your own breathing and instead you stare hard at the hairs on his wrists. It is now that you think for the first time: *I am neither an especially smart person, nor an especially talented person. It is not that I am lazy or that I haven't found the right path or that I've just made a couple of mistakes. I am average, and perhaps not even that, and there is nothing I can do to fix it.* You wish desperately, again, to be the short grey-haired woman in the frame on the desk; the woman with a job and a husband and certainty about who she is. It is now that you do start crying, silently. Mr Hughes inhales deeply before speaking again, and you wonder how often he has to make someone like you confront the reality of themself.

'. . . our past endeavours tend to play a big role in these things and, I think, unfortunately, perhaps some doors may already be closed to you.'

Seventeen years old – February 4th

Your January module results are not good. You tell your parents over dinner and your father, blithe and unobservant, says, 'Well done, chum!' and your mother says nothing. You watch her spoon butternut squash soup into her mouth. Later that evening she calls you to the kitchen and says quietly, 'I want so desperately to be proud of you.'

Seventeen years old – February 27th

Something is wrong with your toenail. The skin on the side of your left big toe is dark red and angry and painful to the touch. You can't find the edge of your nail – it seems to have got lost in the skin. You try to use your thumbnail to ease the toenail out from the swollen cushion of flesh but the pain makes you flinch.

Seventeen years old – February 28th

More skin has turned red, and when you hit your toe on the edge of the bed your foot detonates with pain.

Seventeen years old – March 6th

There is a large patch of scarlet down one side of the nail and the entirety of your toe feels tight. When you apply pressure, yellow oozes out. You Google 'ingrown toenail' and you feel nauseous at the images of discoloured alien welts. You close the laptop. You wrap your toe in a bandage and slide it into your school sock. You contemplate the wrongness of your body.

Seventeen years old – March 15th

'So, Joan was supposed to book the hotel for the women's lunch, and she didn't, so that's one more bit of nonsense I have to deal with.'

'Why didn't she?'

'Oh, the usual. More nonsense with her son, who has still not managed to extricate himself from Molly.'

'So he's still mollified.'

She smiles. 'You were so funny, when you were little.'

She pulls out of the supermarket car park. One of her sleeves slides up her arm.

'What's that?'

'Hmm?'

'That, on your arm.'

On the inside of her upper right arm there is a small pink-red dot, slightly raised. You've never noticed it before.

'Oh, that's just a birthmark. My brother had one too, but on his leg. We used to pretend they were the sources of our secret twin powers.'

Your mother does not mention her brother often, and on the anniversary of his death each year she stays in her room. You look down at the small bottle of hand sanitizer she keeps in the car door pocket, and you think about how she never lets you take the unwrapped mints from the Chinese takeaway, how she would always wash your new clothes before letting you wear them as a child, how she is never late to book a dental check-up. You wonder if she feels betrayed by him – if his delay in getting tested was an affront to her fastidiousness, if, in that moment, he became unknowable, someone who had, until then, seemed like an extension of her own self. You look back at the small red blob.

'It's cute.'

'I think it's called a strawberry nevus.'

'Ah, the sister of Ben.'

The force of her laugh shocks you. It's been a while since you have heard her laugh like this – long and prolonged and slow to fade. She shakes her head. The two of you sit in silence, and you watch the tendons in her wrist move as she works the gear stick in the small black Toyota Yaris. She speaks first.

'Are you sure you want to go away next year?'

You think of the girl in the tartan skirt and the turtle-neck: 'Yes.'

'Have you decided where?'

You sigh. So far, you have received one offer and two rejections, although you haven't relayed this information. You sigh again. 'I don't know,' and you see her jaw stiffen slightly. Your not knowing things has always irritated her. You try again.

'I think I've ruined it and it's too late for me to go anywhere good.'

She doesn't say anything, but her jaw relaxes. She frowns slightly at the road. When she pulls on to the kerb outside your house she doesn't let go of the wheel for a while.

'You know, there are lots of things from my life I wish I could change.'

You wonder if you might cry. Your voice is ashy. 'Me too.'

She reaches over and squeezes your knee. 'We can fix this.'

'Yeah?'

'Yes. Even if it's too late to get you an offer for somewhere you like now, we can get you to resit your January exams, and then do well in your summer ones. We can get you something good. There are options. You don't have to feel stuck.'

'OK.'

'You might not be happy right now, but that doesn't mean you won't be happy later.'

'OK.'

'I know that you can be great.'

You swallow. 'Yeah?'

'Yes. We just have to get you through these exams, OK?'

'OK.'

She smiles. 'OK?'

'OK.'

She laughs and squeezes your knee again. She takes the key out of the ignition. 'OK.'

Seventeen years old – March 19th

You see him, standing at the bar. You nudge Rachael, who unfastens herself from a conversation with a handsome boy in your year called David who is notably talented at cricket but, as far as you can tell, incredibly stupid. She looks irritated at the interruption. You gesture to the man at the bar. 'What about him?'

'What about him?'

'Do you think he's good-looking?'

She grimaces. 'Ew, no, but you do you.' She turns back to David, and you go and stand closer to the bar.

He has dark, matted hair and when you are close you notice there is no stubble on his cheeks, not even the deep pores you see on the chins of other men. His skin is smooth, like the Cabbage Patch doll you had as a child. Its name was Broccoli. It had two plaits of yarn and sunken eyes and it made you wish that your name was Broccoli.

He's slim but his hips and ass are wide; his thighs seem glued together and then his legs diverge at the knees like a Cheestring. His lower half is feminine and his face is cherubic, with observable cheekbones and soft jowls and lips like sleeping mole rats. You wonder if it would be odd to tell him that he is beautiful, or whether the oddness of it could be intriguing. You wonder if for you to say it on the grounds that it could be intriguing would negate the intrigue. You decide to say nothing. You buy two drinks and you go and stand at his elbow, expectantly. A friend of his says, 'Donal, you have a visitor,' and nods in your direction. Donal turns, notices you.

'Is one of those for me?' he says, then smiles.

Seventeen years old – March 29th

You meet him for a drink on a wet night. Before you arrive at the bar you receive two texts. One from Rachael, saying, **Relax. Be yourself. Don't be weird xx** and one from him, saying, **Don't blow away! X**. It is in this moment that you know you will sleep with him.

He studies music at university, but he's taking a year out to focus on his band.

'We've played quite a few gigs, mostly local, a lot of weddings. We're trying to get some things at festivals and stuff but it's hard, cos Andy, our bassist, got a spot studying medicine in Manchester, which, like, I mean, it's cool. I mean, I *get* it, you know? It's just, if we keep swapping members round people aren't going to take us seriously, you know? Plus with every new member comes a new suggestion for what the name should be, which is so stupid, and it's like, guys, the name doesn't matter—'

'You could be called Local Anaesthetic.'

A pause. He makes you repeat what you said. You do, hesitantly. There is another pause.

'Oh, because of Andy. Right.'

He buys the first round, you the second. You match his drink orders, so you have beer, then another beer, then whisky. When you suggest doing shots he smiles and says, 'So you're a party girl, huh?' and you're not sure why this makes you feel as good as it does.

In his room you undress hurriedly, careful to slide your tights over your foot in a way that doesn't interfere with the taupe-coloured bandage on your toe. Your hair has gone frizzy and lank in the moist air and you touch it repeatedly, trying not to panic. His cock is squat. You've never seen one in real life. You are naked and lying on the bed and trying to keep your breasts from hanging off either side of your torso like blood bags. You think perhaps the short thickness of his cock is something you shouldn't dwell on, because what do you know about what makes a good cock? He might be wondering at the great pale expanse of your abdomen, or your fuzzy hair, splayed on the pillow like a spider plant.

You put your hand between his legs and start to stroke it. There's no music on, no sound at all apart from his breathing, which you are relieved to hear grow heavier and damper. The only other sound is the occasional sleigh-bell tinkling of the bracelet on your wrist. You wonder if you ought to try and instigate his going inside you, and you think about leading him there by his cock, like a dog on a leash. You think this thought away.

Eventually his penis, now as substantial and rounded as a tube of roll-on deodorant, is an angry, dark shade, and he leans over you and pushes his fingers into the fold between your legs. It feels wrong. An errant pubic hair you didn't manage to shave off has got caught up in his hand and as he thrusts his fingers in the hair gets tugged at the root and your eyes water. Your insides feel arid and tight and like there's no give – like trying to push a toy car over an unyielding carpet. When he pulls his fingers out you are relieved. He reaches over to a drawer on his bedside table. You pre-empt his actions and say, 'Don't worry, I'm on the pill,' and being able to say this makes you feel mature, sexually experienced, even though it was Rachael who went to the walk-in clinic to get it for you. His hand stops its trajectory, and he nods, says, 'OK.' You think he looks slightly put out by your having spoken, and you wonder if his arousal is dependent on your silence. He bends over and puts his lips against yours – they feel like raw chicken fillets. You imagine the two of you getting into a rhythm a couple of times a week – drinks, holding hands as you walk to his flat, him putting on some music and the two of you getting to know each other's bodies, you learning how to accommodate his fingers, him learning that you would like him to look at you as you touch him, to show you that you're doing it right.

You imagine him inviting you to dinner with his parents. You'll buy something flattering and inoffensive and you will tell the assistant in the changing room that tonight is a big deal. His mother will think you're pretty and his father will think you're charming. He'll squeeze your knee under the table and the sex afterwards will be more frantic than usual. You'll tighten your arms around him while he thumps his hips against yours. Your bodies will be hungry and energetic, because the dinner and the well-cooked beef and the chocolates that come with the coffee will have reminded you both that you are at the start of something.

You imagine the two of you reminiscing on your first time, joking about how little you really knew each other. You imagine him saying that you looked beautiful and you will say you were worried about your hair and he will laugh good-naturedly because this was the last thing he cared about, and anyway, your hair always looks good, and maybe then you'll tell him about your misshapen toe under its bandage, which by now will be renewed and healthy. He'll grimace, but even this will be with affection, because he wishes you had just told him at the time, so he could have made sure not to nudge it with his foot.

He nudges your toe with his foot. The toe throbs. You try not to focus on it, but you're also worried about the dry sting you felt when his fingers went inside you – what will happen when the squirming tardigrade between his legs pushes its way in? He's lowering himself on to you and into you now and – it hurts. He isn't all the way in – you glance down and see two inches of angry flesh sticking out of you – and it hurts. He tries to push himself in further, and then he glances up and something in your face makes him stop. You tell him to keep going and he says, 'It's kind of hard when you look like you're in pain,' and so you try to look calm, but it's like something is being forced between two pieces held together with Velcro, and with every push more of you comes apart with a crackling rip.

You inhale sharply and he stops. He pulls out. He lies down next to you with a sigh and you spend the next ten minutes furiously moving your fingers up and down his cock in the navy air and when that fails you lick it, you lick it up and down and you take it into your throat until you feel the tug of a gag in your oesophagus like a fishing line, but still you keep going. You wish there was music on to cover the sound of the croaking hiccup noises coming from inside you. Eventually he says, 'I should get some sleep,' and he turns on to his side, away from you. You stare at the damp smudges in the corners of the ceiling, wide awake. You imagine the two of you lying side by side on the grass in summer, his fingers tickling your palm.

Seventeen years old – March 30th

You text him, telling him you had a nice time, asking to see him again. While you wait for a reply you open your history textbook. You read a few pages and then open your laptop and watch a clip on YouTube: 'How to give a great blowjob'. An attractive American with golden-brown hair demonstrates on a banana. She licks it up and down, then takes it into her mouth. She explains how to breathe through your nose so you don't gag. You check your phone – nothing. You watch the video again.

Seventeen years old – April 1st

Your mother slams the door of the oven. She turns to you.

'Has he replied?'

You look at your phone. You texted your father eighteen minutes ago.

'No.'

She sighs, then wrenches the door open again. She pulls out the baking tray full of pasta and cheese and the smaller baking tray full of carrots and onions and courgette. She starts to spoon food on to two plates, violently.

'I don't see how it's so difficult for him. I don't see what he could possibly be doing that means he can't be home in time for dinner. I can't believe he is in such high demand that being home in time to shovel food into his mouth is beyond his capabilities.'

You pour two glasses of orange juice. She rubs her temples.

'Never marry a man just because he seems kind, OK? It might seem like kindness is the most important thing, but kindness has an expiry date, and then all you're left with is stupid' – a pause – 'and inconsiderate.'

You put a chunk of carrot into your mouth. You chew slowly.

Your father comes home thirty-five minutes later. Your mother opens the door and does not say hello to him. She turns and goes upstairs. He comes into the kitchen and winks at you.

'Hi, sweetie.'

You stare at him. You gesture to the oven where the

leftovers are. He walks over, opens the door, looks in, then closes it again.

'No thanks, pet. I'm not hungry.'

'Where were you?'

'What's that? Oh, sorry, love. Work crisis, it ran on. I'm going to go grab a shower.' He leans over and kisses your scalp, then leaves. You take the baking tray out of the oven and stand at the counter, forking blackened bits of pasta into your mouth.

Seventeen years old – April 14th

You are sitting on the floor of the Topshop changing room. Outside in the antechamber Rachael and Bethany and Charlie are talking and joking and admiring each other's choices. It's Rachael's eighteenth birthday, and one month before exams start. You are halfway inside a pair of checked trousers a size too small. The checks blur and pixelate as the fabric is stretched. The lights are impossibly bright – they throw silver rings around your pupils when you look yourself in the eye. There is a sheen of slime on your upper lip and your cheeks are red and distended. You stand up and try to pull the trousers a little further up your legs but the ridge of flesh at the top of your thighs seems solid and immovable. You struggle against the starched fabric until you hear the pop of a thread snapping and at this your grip slackens and you lean against the wall.

You check your phone – Donal never replied to your text

and your whole body hums with resignation. You pull down the sleeve of your school jumper and wad it into your mouth and bite down hard, as hard as you can, until your teeth hurt and your jaw aches and your closed eyes bulge. The polyester fabric comes away dark with saliva and with two semicircular ridges of teeth marks.

The four of you go straight from the shopping centre to the train station. The journey takes an hour and a half, one train and then another train. The three girls grab four seats with a table but when you go to sit down Charlie places her hand on the seat next to her. She smiles at you, pantomime-villain contrite, and says, 'Mind if I keep this free? I hurt my knee at hockey and might need to put my leg up.' You sit alone, occasionally twisted at the waist and leaning over to take part in the conversation, mostly staring out the window, pulling loose skin from the sides of your finger-nails. You think about how you will escape all of this soon. You flatten your hand on your thigh; count the fingers and thumb. Five months. You wish your hand was like your mother's, one finger short, because then it would be one month less.

In the hostel room there are bunk beds, and you are grateful for their structural inclusivity. You do not take a shower, and as you all sit in a circle on the gritty parquet floor, passing around a Ribena bottle filled with vodka, you can smell the tang of yourself. The others have all bought variations on the same outfit and they realize this with a discordant squeal of delight. Charlie asks you to take a photo of them – and then eight more photos of them. You are positioned around the room: in the doorway, by the window, wobbling on the thin duvet on one of the single beds. You take another swig from the bottle, then another, until the smell of yourself bothers you less, until you stop accidentally catching sight of your reflection in the smudgy mirror. The right side of your face is saggy and drooping and a surprise every time you see it.

The hostel pub has fake graffiti on the walls and picnic tables inside. You are swallowing shots of pink stuff that tastes like the bubblegum mouthwash you were sometimes bought as a child. You keep going up to the bar to buy more, because the barman has long, curly, blondish hair and stubble and one pronounced knob of bone on his shoulder that doesn't match the other side. You think he is beautiful, so you buy more drinks. The other girls are already drunk and bored. Rachael is taking photos of the room and Bethany is texting her boyfriend and Charlie is staring at an elderly man sitting at another table. 'Oh, that makes me so sad,' she slurs. 'He's so old and alone and pathetic. He must be so lonely. I'd hate to be old and lonely, wouldn't you?' She looks at you, and something about her chemical-green eyes makes you think she can see into your old, lonely future. You look away.

You have always wondered at the strange fetishization of the elderly; what makes them more prone to loneliness than you or anyone else? You don't say anything. You drink the bubblegum mouthwash and watch the barman.

An hour later the others want to go to McDonald's. You decide to stay. Rachael says, 'Are you sure? Just come with us – get some food,' but you shake your head and she's too drunk to try harder. They stumble out.

You know that this is a turning point, that this is a moment of some significance, that this is you setting yourself apart from the others. You are happy to sit by yourself, like the old man, but it's more important that it's you because you are young and young women sitting alone in bars mean something different. You have a whisky and coke in front of you, and you cross and uncross your legs and then cross them again and you sway gently on the lacquered bench and you sip the drink and you watch the barman. He's wearing a vest top. You want to poke that raised lump of bone. He looks sinewy and healthy and he has a thin upper lip. You imagine him coming over and sitting across from you, two drinks in his hands. You imagine becoming aware of his knee between your knees. Maybe he would shift slightly in his seat and slide his leg forward and to the right so it was pressed tight against your inner thigh. Maybe after some time he would lean forward and lift himself up and kiss you, smiling while he did it so his thin upper lip was stretched thinner and you could feel his hard front teeth against your mouth. Maybe he'd say he wanted to do that from the moment you walked in.

He's drying a glass and staring at the television in the corner. It's playing a music video, but it doesn't correspond to the song that's playing on the speakers. You want to catch the ankles of the woman on the screen and make her step back and forth in time with the thumps of the music. You finish your drink – the dregs in the bottom of the glass taste like the smell of paint. You stumble up to the bar and lean against it and wait for him to notice you. He looks at you and says something but it's too loud and you can't hear him but he's pouring two shots. His upper lip has almost completely disappeared and his name is foreign but he speaks like you. His name is Jacob, but with a 'Yah'. *Yahcob*. You make a show of trying to pronounce it, stopping after the first syllable each time to laugh self-effacingly so he knows that you know that you're bad at this.

'What are you thinking about?'

You hiccup. 'I don't know.'

You hope he'll press you on it.

'I need to get out of here,' he says. 'A few more months and then I'm moving somewhere else.'

A burp rises in your throat. You swallow it back down. 'Do you ever think about how you might secretly be immune to something?'

He frowns. 'What?'

'Like, some horrible disease. What if your body was immune to it – if you got the disease but then your body just, like, healed itself. You'd never know you were special.'

'I guess.'

'Would you want to know? If it meant your body could provide a cure, but it might also mean you had to undergo tests and procedures and stuff. Would you still want to know?'

He's still frowning at you. 'I don't know.'

'And like, what's the limit, you know? How many procedures or experiments would you be willing to go through for the world to have a cure? Would you die? Would you be willing to die so countless people could live?'

He looks at his drink, bored. 'I don't know, man. Funnily enough I don't like to think about me dying.'

You look at him and wonder what's going to happen next. 'No?'

Seventeen years old – May 3rd

Your alarm goes off. You've been awake for hours. You don't sleep much at all now. You walk to the bathroom with your arms wrapped around yourself. On the toilet you bite your fingers and stare at your swollen toe, still encased in its bandage. Hard, painful shits tear their way out of you and load up in the bowl. You check and make sure nothing else has fallen out with them, then flush. You stand at the sink and look in the mirror. Your eyes are red. Cold air whistles around inside you, chills your insides. You have the leftovers of a large red spot on your cheek. It's healing slowly.

You hold your hands under the tap until the water gives off steam and the skin on your fingers is repentant and stinging. You notice there is a long black hair coming out of your chin. You stroke it, then start rootling in your father's toilet bag to find a razor. His toilet bag is large, dark green, smells like ripe fruit. You push aside a bottle of cologne and an empty hotel shower gel to find the orange and black razor. You hear a crinkling sound as your hand brushes against something. You let go of the razor and pull out something else. It's a silver pill packet, rectangular. It has four plastic bubbles, two of which have already been burst and emptied. The remaining two have pale-blue, diamond-shaped pills inside. You grip the pill packet in your hand, then walk to your room and type 'blue diamond shaped pills' into Google. You stare at the screen. It is two weeks until exams start.

PART II

Seventeen years old – May 16th (today)

You wake to a hot and itchy wetness between your thighs. You wriggle on the sheets, feeling the fabric of your pyjama bottoms get pulled taut around your legs and made warm by what has happened. You remember who you are in increments, and you wish you could sleep for a month, a year, five years. It's the day of your A-level history exam.

Your bed sits low to the ground, and so you roll off the mattress and on to your hands and knees on the floor. You stay like that for a moment, curled in child's pose. You breathe in, and you wonder if it's your body you can smell, or the world.

The bathroom is dark and cool like a church vestibule. The blue toilet seat feels matte against your ass and the floor is tiled with yellow and beige linoleum – the borders between the colours indistinct and puffy, like a sepia-toned landscape or the mustard-coloured insulation that lines the attic. When you were little you liked to pretend the toilet was a small airship; its engine powered by whatever plopped or slid along the sides of the bowl.

When you look into the gusset of your pants you are confronted with a small, glistening blood clot. It stares at you, and you stare back, shocked by the subdued horror of it. You giggle and it seems to mirror you, its embers wiggling. You put your finger below the gusset – it feels humid – and press upwards. The nucleus of the clot splits slightly and when you let go it re-forms and rocks back and forth, keeping time with your breathing.

You know the normal thing to do would be to flush it, to peel the clot off the fabric with toilet paper and flush it away like they do with dead goldfish on American sitcoms. (You've never had a goldfish; have never wanted the responsibility.) You tense for a moment and listen to the splashes of the airship. You hold your breath and keep still and try to detect the clot's absence inside you, if there's a new, cool chasm somewhere in your bloodstream to prove that you're missing a piece. You wish you could take the clot and use it to plug that other perforation deep inside you, the one that whistles with cold air, that you are never not aware of these days. You shake away the bad thoughts. Not today.

The circumference of the clot is about that of a blueberry – not the largest menstrual clot you've shed, but not insignificant either. You marvel at your body's ability to create and then reject it so willingly, to turn something so delicate and glossy into waste matter. Where do all the discarded scraps of people end up? You take a piece of toilet roll and scoop the clot on to the paper. You whisper, 'Hello, goldfish,' and stand. You ball the paper violently and throw it into the bowl. You read somewhere once that the body replaces all its red blood cells every 120 days. If that's the case, all the dark red inside you is still dirty and unclean. You flush the toilet and walk to your bedroom. The sunset-coloured chimera of your big toe palpitates merrily with each step.

★

You have begun to derive a morbid satisfaction from being so far from where you ought to be, so obstinately different from what a nearly eighteen-year-old woman should be, should look like. You often go to Rachael's house on a Friday evening, and while she files her nails or tries on the padded bras she's just bought, you sit on her bed, dressed in your old white t-shirt with the yellow marks in the armpits, and watch her. You use your fingers to cram cold slices of turkey and ham into your mouth, and as she turns in the mirror you notice the lines of her ribcage or shoulder blades sharpen into focus.

With her fingers adjusting the pastel-toned frilly cup, she'll say, 'What about this one?' Sometimes you grab a piece of paper from the printer on her desk and scrawl a number on it with black felt-tip. She'll throw up her hands in mock-outrage, cry, 'A six?! This is a disgrace!' And you'll say, 'It's a competitive category, I'm afraid, and I just don't think the lavender has the delicacy of form that we're expecting.' She'll nod solemnly and say, 'If we don't have honesty, the whole integrity of the sport is compromised.' She'll take the bra off and throw it forcefully into the bag, her uncaged breasts jiggling at the movement. You feel relief at the vast gulf between your bodies, how you harbour no resentment towards her beauty. You're an aberration, and because it's not your fault, why would you try to be anything else?

You stand in front of the bedroom mirror, first face on and then sideways. You run your hands over the firm dome of your belly and then you hunch forward until your breasts rest on top of it. The light catches and shades all the dips

83

and defects of your skin. You place your hands on your abdomen and point your chin downwards. The protrusions of your breasts and head and nose cast wavy shadows over your torso, like curves of coastal erosion. You look like a monster. You force out a laugh.

Midway up one leg you abandon the task of putting on tights to scratch at the dry skin under your arm. The straight black line of nylon across the white, etiolated flesh of your leg reminds you of an Oreo after you bifurcate it. It's going to be another warm day, but you haven't shaved your legs and your calves are bristly with black, the hair thicker and darker than the downy hairs at the tops of your thighs. You like how your leg hairs poke through the pores in the fabric of the tights – sometimes you joke that you're not wearing tights at all, and depending on who you say it to, sometimes you get a laugh.

Your school skirt is dark grey and pleated and it's customary to roll the waistband to make it shorter. Sometimes you roll it as many as eight times and the band sits like a string of fat sausages around your middle. Before you started secondary school you might have thought it was better to wear clothes that were comfortable, or that flattered your figure, but you have since learned that how you look or feel is largely irrelevant to reputation. After all, there are plenty of unattractive people who are popular, and plenty of attractive people who aren't. It's more important not to draw attention to yourself, even if it means you can feel the cold air encroaching on the pillows of your upper thighs. Sometimes you wonder if an ugly girl's popularity lies in her perceived ambivalence to the way she looks, but you also wonder if maybe the popular girls are just the ones who are fun to spend time with.

On the kitchen counter there's a green Post-it note with 'Good luck today! xo' written on it, and a bowl filled with a beige lump of porridge. It has turned solid and dense, has the consistency of dried glue. It has already been sitting for about twenty minutes, left to dry and solidify while you dawdled upstairs. Cooking your breakfast is the last thing your mother does before leaving for work – still the dental practice – and the porridge she buys is the unsweetened sort. You hate the taste of it, the cold, rubbery, polenta texture of it, but you have a ritual.

Every morning you run a spoon around the edge of the slab and wedge it out of the bowl. It always comes away cleanly. You wrap it in bumblebee-printed kitchen roll. Then comes the disposal. You can't put the porridge in the kitchen bin or even into the wheelie bin outside – your mother has a habit of foraging through to retrieve the recyclables your father ignored, and the thought of her finding it fills you with dread, of her saying, 'What is this? Why on earth have you done this? How long have you been doing this?' or of your father, trying to make a joke to smooth things over: 'It can't taste that bad! Now if *I* was making the porridge, then we'd have a problem, right, love?'

For a while you would carry the porridge to the edge of the small strip of garden at the back of the house. You would throw the lump over the fence and into the dense foliage beyond. This seemed to work – until the morning it got stuck on a low tree branch and floated, conspicuous, like a fat, moulting pigeon. Bits of it fell off and spattered against the fence, and you had to fetch a clothes hanger to try and knock it down like a piñata, your anxiety levels rising. Since then you have been more careful, and instead you mummify the porridge and carry it to school in your blazer pocket. You dispose of it in a bin in the school car park. It seems like the most straightforward solution.

You put the embalmed porridge in the pocket of your blazer, hanging from the banister. In the pocket there's a breadcrumb trail of hair slides and pennies. In the other pocket there's an apple from the week before. Now that you're on study leave your blazer goes unattended for days, and the partially eaten apple has large patches of brown. You put it to your mouth and nibble a bit off – it has a meaty consistency, like dried turkey. You roll the chunk around your mouth before swallowing. You hold the apple to your face and sniff: it smells like a gym changing room. You put it back in your pocket. You still don't like apples, but you like having something to hold in your hand and work at while you're at school. You like the functionality of an apple, how eating it feels akin to doing a crossword or writing an email.

The green Post-it is stuck to the bally wool of your jumper sleeve. 'Good luck today! xo'. You read it until the words become meaningless.

Good luck today! xo

Good luck today! Ex Oh

Good luck today ex oh

Good luck today kiss hug

Goodlucktodaykisshug

Goodlucktodaykisshuggoodlucktodaykisshuggoodlucktodaykisshug

You go back upstairs, rubbing the soles of your feet repeatedly over the worn patches in the carpet.

Your history textbook is lying open on your desk. Your history teacher has a mantra: event, cause, motive, consequence. Scott once asked, 'Are cause and motive not the same thing?' and everyone laughed, but nobody answered. Event and cause and motive and consequence, your teacher says, are the keys to answering a question effectively. Next to the book is a practice paper, face down. You flick it over and scan the instructions on the cover. You thumb idly through the textbook. Event and cause and motive and consequence. You still think about touching the immediate hardness of Scott's penis through his thin school trousers. You wish your friendship had survived the summer. You wish you'd got to feel his overbite pressed against your lips.

You close the book. You go to the window and close the curtains. You get into bed and pull the duvet over you; the cover is green and dotted with images of wild flowers. Some nights you like to pretend it's an actual flowerbed and you have to sleep under a thick layer of soil and bluebells. Once there, all you have to do is stay quiet and regulate your breathing. You reach one hand down and scratch at your swollen and painful toe. You close your eyes.

You have always suspected you would flourish at the centre of a crisis. You think you could be brave and silent and dignified if confronted with trauma. You're jealous of the people who get this opportunity: the girl in the year above who had arrived home one day to find her mother surrounded by empty paracetamol sheets and frothing at the mouth; the boy who's just returned to school following a much-publicized battle with leukaemia; the girl who got knocked over on a council estate and appeared in the halls with her leg frozen in a white cast. The cast was soon covered in drawings and flowers and games of Xs and Os – it had seemed to you that the cast had provided her with a vast currency of new friendships. These people always wound up being OK, but from then on they were permanently marked as noteworthy and special. They were people to be spoken about in the context of their bravery.

When you were eight years old two English sisters had disappeared – the younger one the same age as you. They were taken from outside a petrol station near Birmingham, and their disappearance was your first real awareness of a news story, of a nation united in a collective, abstract sadness. In the picture that hovered at the newscasters' temples the girls wore matching red jumpers and were curled up on a clashing red sofa. They had huge blue eyes, and matching overlaps in their front teeth. You remember your mother, rapt on the sofa, gripping a mug. You remember the sound of the spoon clinking against the ceramic. You remember her murmuring, 'Those poor girls' – and then a pause – 'and so beautiful.'

The girls had never been found, and when you find yourself coveting trauma you think of them and try to think better thoughts. You then reprimand yourself for using them as a jumping-off point for self-improvement. You wonder what the younger sister would look like now. You roll on to your side and try to get comfortable.

Before now you were never sure of the specifics of the event that would vault you into the same category as the two girls and the boy from school, now revered. You used to think you would like it to be something you could keep secret for a while, something that could lurk behind your vacant expression. Your eyes would have a sort of wet sincerity to them, and your smile would be always close-mouthed. You would suffer quietly, until one day it would all come out. You might be in the school canteen, spooning something soupy and lumpy into your mouth. Perhaps there would be some triggering statement or raucous laugh or complicit nudge from Rachael and suddenly your secret would prove too heavy. She would look at you and sense it. She would say, 'What's wrong, buttercup?' and you would no longer be capable of stoicism. It would all come out and you would collapse in on yourself like a deflating bouncy castle. Teachers would be informed, the police, maybe – the local press. You would endure all of this, too, with the same smile and unreadable patina in your eyes. You would downplay it, obviously; you would champion your parents and friends, your 'support system', the people that remind you that love vanquishes pain. You can picture a clump of indistinguishable journalists with misshapen teeth chewing on their pens. They would scramble to interview you, and when they thought you couldn't hear them they'd mutter to one another, 'Christ, I can't go home till I get this damn exclusive with fucking Mother Teresa incarnate.'

You would return to school weeks later, with tentative steps – unsteady with your new insights, your new awareness. There would be a collective desire to protect you. You would need space, but also to know that you weren't alone. The wealthy, popular girls would run home to their family dinners of Marks & Spencer sea bass, buoyant with the opportunity to participate in an adult conversation about human suffering. This would be your gift to them. Teachers would offer you deadline extensions, lunch-line privileges, after-class 'chats'. You would nod and smile and say how much you appreciate the kindness but, actually, you just want things to go back to normal. You would walk away and they'd say to each other, 'What a brave girl' – and then, 'and so beautiful.'

The danger of the flowerbed game is that it can sometimes feel like being buried alive; the duvet with its uneven lumps like clods of earth, the sweat from your body oozing into the fabric like cold rain. You imagine the earth and dirt turning to clay in the wet and preserving your stiff limbs. You shake your legs to break the sensation, then stick one arm out the side of the bed. You open your eyes. The exam paper glows white on the desk like a nightlight. You shut your eyes tight again.

Your ringtone wakes you, a polyphonic mimicking of birdsong. Your eyelids peel apart like two fat segments of orange. You turn and look at the clock by your bedside; you've been asleep for two hours. Your sinuses feel plugged and painful and your head hurts. You snake one arm on to the floor and grab your phone.

'Hello?'

Rachael's laughter barrels down the line. 'Have I just woken you up?'

'No.'

'Are you ill?'

You swallow. 'I hope not.'

'OK, little miss sunshine. Did you know that when we visit my gran the last thing she always says right before we leave is, "It's a long time till morning."'

'OK.'

'Bit grim, isn't it? Anyway, seems like something you might say.'

'I suppose.'

'What are you up to? I feel like I've barely seen you since my birthday.'

'I'm not up to anything.'

'Well, great! Want to come in a little early and we can grab lunch before we get metaphorically guillotined by this exam? I've been here since nine and I'm just roving the corridors like Miss Havisham with a pocket full of biros.'

You're not sure if it's the connection or your brain causing the echo of her voice. You close your eyes.

'Hello? You still there?'

You hang up, and the fresh silence is like coming up for air.

You get out of bed sluggishly – your limbs are heavy and your eyes shrivelled like currants. The blood clot in your pants feels like something that happened yesterday and you wish it were; that this day was over. You go to the desk, pointedly not looking at the textbook. Your phone rings again and you stare at it. After what feels like an impossibly long time the phone is still ringing, and you answer.

'Hello?'

'Don't know what happened there. Anyway – you coming in, snookums? We can talk about liberalism in France, and who the fuck the Whigs are, and how many Napoleons is too many Napoleons.'

You sway from one foot to the other. You feel a film of sweat form between your cheek and the phone screen. You say nothing.

'Is something up? You're being weird.'

'I'm not being weird.'

'You're being weird. What the hell is wrong with you?'

You open the desk drawer with one hand and rummage, nudging to one side old receipts and a dirty tissue and a few chewable vitamin C tablets, broken into shrapnel. You pull out the silver sheet containing the blue, diamond-shaped pills. You turn it over and over in your hand, running your thumb over its textures. Everything, you want to say. You want to tell her about the dirty blood inside you, about the whistling hole, about these small pale-blue pills.

'Nothing.'

'C'mon, don't do this.'

'Do what?'

'I'm trying to remember about eighteen different names and fourteen different dates and the difference between France and Italy and also how to spell my own name.'

'Right.'

'I can't also deal with trying to work out if you're having a subdural haematoma.'

'OK.'

'Can you please just be calm and normal? Just come in and eat some undercooked chips with me.'

You count the bubbles on the blister pack, continue swaying, say nothing.

'What is going on with you?'

'Nothing.'

'Right. Great.' Her tone is so irritated now it makes your chest tight.

'OK.'

'OK.'

You assume she will hang up, but when she doesn't, 'OK.'

'You're exhausting sometimes, you know?'

You let your eyes close, lethargic. 'I know.'

'Great. Well as long as you know.'

'OK.'

'Last chance?'

You play the jingle for Calgon washing-machine tablets in your head. Rachael sighs. 'OK. I'll see you later then, yeah?'

'OK.'

'We can go to the park after, see some of the hard brown men with the green heads. Yeah?'

You want to cry. You swallow again, think about speaking. Her voice turns suddenly, blisteringly cold, a tone normally reserved for people who aren't you. 'Right, whatever. See you.' She hangs up, and you are left standing on one foot, the pill packet gripped in your hand, your throat constricted. You take the phone away from your ear, switch it off and set it on the desk. You blink away your tears and nurse the pill packet in your hands like a fledgling. You carry it reverentially downstairs. You slide it into your blazer pocket so it nestles against the porridge, wrapped in kitchen roll.

This has become another daily ritual, as normal as brushing your teeth. Every day you take the pill packet from the sock in the drawer and put it in your pocket. You take it to school. You bring it home. You return it to the drawer. You have been doing this for a fortnight, ever since you found the pills in your father's toilet bag. There is a cupboard in the kitchen filled with tablets: multivitamins and vitamin C and omega 3 and tablets for congestion, diarrhoea, migraine, constipation, hay fever, indigestion, depression, anxiety, insomnia. Your mother lines her tablets up in a row with her breakfast; she encourages you to do the same, but you don't. When you first found the pills in the toilet bag you wondered why they didn't look like the other pills in the cupboard; you wondered why they were hidden.

Since you stole them you sometimes find your father searching. You walk past his room and see him lying on his stomach, one arm wedged under the bed. Sometimes you see him rifling furiously in the bathroom cupboard or trying to surreptitiously slide his hands into every jacket hanging on the coat stand in the hall. A week ago you had stood in the doorway of his room, motionless, watching him peer under the chest of drawers, manoeuvring his arm like an arcade machine claw. He turned his head to the side and noticed you.

'Uh, I was just trying to . . .'

You knew you were supposed to interrupt; with a joke, with a laugh, with a playful dig at how silly he looked with his shirt hoisted around his middle. Instead, you said nothing. You stood there, looking at him, and when he realized he had no way of finishing the sentence the silence gaped with surprised emptiness, like when your foot expects there to be one more step at the top of the staircase.

You like watching him search frantically. You like to see him so unreservedly bewildered, to think that if you wanted to you could reach out and lift his confusion from his skin like the fabric of a thin jumper. You like seeing someone else feel how you seem to feel most of the time: confused, dislodged. When he looks at you, you can see your own expression, mirrored. You wonder if he knows how it feels to get everything wrong.

You take the pill packet out of your pocket. You tap the

four clear bubbles with your finger, lingering over the two that have been burst. You place your thumb cautiously under one of the two remaining pills. You push upwards, and the silver foil snaps like a wishbone. The diamond sits, freshly exposed. You hold it up to your eye and read the code printed on it. You think of dry crackers, salt, pasta shells, and your mouth fills with saliva. You put the pill on your tongue and swallow forcefully, once, twice. You think about it making its way through you. You wonder what happens now.

Liberalism was more successful in France than other European countries in the period 1815–1914.

You read the practice question over and over again, then flick through the paper and read the alternatives – none of the topics seem to have anything to do with you. You try for a moment to think of any history class from the last five months – you think of the coppery highlights in Rachael's hair, the tiny cannons on Mr O'Brien's tie, the day a wasp flew in and all the girls screamed. You shake your head and turn the paper over so a blank white sheet looks up at you. This seems more appropriate. You pry open your laptop – the lid was tacked down with old skin flakes and a grey sludge made of hairspray and dust. The screen lights up with the web page you were looking at last night.

DO I HAVE HIV?
LEARN ABOUT 11 EARLY SIGNS OF INFECTION.

You move your finger over the mouse pad until the cursor is positioned over the red X in the corner. You click down and the words disappear. Not today.

★

Your mother has left you the car to drive to school. She usually only does this on days when it's raining. She walks to work in her black Clarks shoes with the sturdy beige soles and her navy jacket, holding her black umbrella with the white flowers. Hanging from the wing mirror of the black Toyota is a small blue pillow on a blue ribbon. It was a gift from your mother's colleague when she returned to work. It has words embroidered on it in white thread: *Born free, now I'm expensive.* Once a week she uses a cordless vacuum cleaner to clean the seats. When you climb in, your smell mingles with citrus air freshener and the synthetic smell of the upholstery. The car always feels, smells, like a courtesy car. The dashboard lights up with the time.

11:48

You twist the key further till the engine hums. The front tyre rubs against the kerb as you pull away.

You've had a part-time job in a local supermarket for eight months. Your boss is a middle-aged man with tan-coloured gunk under his fingernails, like peanut butter, and when he puts a hand on your shoulder you can't help but stare at his fingers and feel the familiar bubbling of queasiness. You imagine him sliding one digit along your lower lip and into your mouth, making you taste the sticky thickness. During your shifts he sits in his office, watching downloads of TV programmes you don't watch, but that you pretend to watch to keep the conversation in harmless territory. He'll call your name and say, 'Seen this week's yet?' and you'll smile and nod. He'll say, 'What did you think?' and sometimes you'll say, 'Bit slow, wasn't it?' or 'That ending was something else.' He'll say, 'It needed more dragons,' and you'll laugh for a moment too long. You enjoy the low-risk thrill that comes from being pointlessly dishonest – it's like you are making him ridiculous in some way, like when a stranger in a cafe rolls their eyes at you as a young mother struggles to quiet her screaming baby. You feel the warmth of being superior, of being responsible for another's exclusion.

Your boss refers to everyone as 'man': 'Gotta be in on time, man'; 'Your shift's not over yet, man'; 'Here, man, will you give me a hand?' You wonder if he knows that he is a non-person, that to you and the other staff members his existence is nothing but a mild inconvenience for sixteen hours a week. Andrea, one of your colleagues, calls him Keith, which isn't his name. He seems to you like a low hum in the background or a safety demonstration on a short-haul flight. You wonder if he knows his teeth are too small for his gums; that their mustard shade makes you queasy. You wonder if he ever tries to clean his fingernails, or if he goes to bars at the weekend and places those peanut butter hands on someone's exposed knee or shoulder. You walk past his office. He's rotating slowly in his swivel chair. On the screen two men are fighting on a clifftop.

'You working today, man?'

'No. I'm filling in the rota.'

'Nice one,' and he keeps his head facing you while his body turns back to the screen, like an owl. 'Though I feel like you're not doing too many shifts, that fair to say? Might want to think about pulling your weight a bit.'

You shrug. He gestures at the computer screen.

'You watch this week's episode yet?'

You shake your head.

'It's pretty good – could use a few more dragons, though.'

You laugh. You nod. You look at the black biro he's using to dig under one fingernail. You scratch at your torso, imagining an impenetrable wall of muscle under your jumper. The jingle for Thirst Pockets kitchen towels plays in your head. You keep walking.

The back room of the shop is windowless. The walls are lined with steel shelving loaded up with boxes of chocolate bars and sweets and crisps. There's a small cracked mirror hanging over a bin, and a single stool pulled up to the counter. Mary, another colleague, is sitting on it. Mary is English and in her early thirties and has, in your opinion, undeservedly symmetrical features. She has wide-set eyes and long, slightly wavy hair that she wears in a plait down her back. The gross injustice of her looks is balanced by the sound of her voice; an abrasive screech you brace in reaction to. She's staring at her phone screen and sighing so heavily that you imagine her skin turning red, then blue, and her collapsing to the floor with a thud. You consider trying to step backwards out of the storeroom, undetected.

'All right, love?'

Her voice has a wild oscillation in pitch, like a cartoon donkey's bray. Every word is painfully over-emphasized, and you wonder if she took elocution lessons as a child, if she had aspirations of being a newsreader before she became crass and dull. You are always polite to her, not because it's good to be polite but because you think you can sense a rigid kernel of violence in her. Something about the tightness of her plait or the way she clenches her fists when your boss is unreasonable makes you think impoliteness might be met with physical force, or public screaming.

'Hi, Mary.'

She looks at her phone again – the plait twists and coils like a snake with the force of her head turn. She sighs again. She angles the phone towards you and you take a reluctant step closer.

'That's my boyfriend.'

You make a show of peering at the photo. 'Oh?'

'He died a couple of weeks ago.'

'Oh.'

You concentrate on the pixelated image of the round man in the red football shirt, hoping your attentive looking will negate the need to say anything else.

'And I know – I *know* – that we hadn't even known each other that long. It'd only been a couple of weeks, right? But you know when you just know?'

Her accent is a strange mix of excessively rounded vowels and the complete abandonment of some consonants. It makes you wonder if she's trying to hide that she's posh, or trying to hide that she's not posh. You nod.

'He was just the most decent man. It's been so hard trying to come to terms with losing him.'

So 'ard. Loo-sing.

'And of course, I wasn't even able to go to the fucking funeral because of that fucking uptight bitch. His fucking uptight bitch of a wife. You know he was going to leave her?'

You nod again, in what you hope is a sympathetic way.

'I've been getting better at thinking about him. It's getting less painful, you know?'

You nod.

'I visited the graveyard yesterday. For the first time.'

Your mother keeps two bottles of plant food in the boot of her car. She goes to her brother's grave unaccompanied, and never says that that is where she's going. You visit the grave rarely. The last time had been following a trip to the cinema with your father, and you had asked to turn in as he drove past the cemetery gates. The grave had a planter full of yellow and orange gladioli sitting on it, and as you stood there you pictured your mother, bent over, face red and arms sore, manoeuvring one of the huge green cartons.

Mary sighs and reaches for the end of her plait. She holds it between her fingers, contemplative and wistful.

'He used to love playing with my hair. He'd always tell me I had more hair than anyone he'd ever met.'

You murmur in assent and she looks up at you, expectant. The curling ends of her plait beckon at you.

'Would you like me to do your hair?'

She hums gently and off-key as you try to slide your fingers through the waves, often encountering resistance. You wonder if she ever brushes it, or just thrusts it into the same tight plait every morning, using muscle memory. The hair at the roots looks slightly wet, and you wonder if her hair gets greasy quickly, or if she washes it infrequently. When you find a large tat midway down she says, 'There's some product in my bag, that'll help,' and you go to her bright yellow, quilted shoulder bag and find a pink can with a push nozzle. You squirt some soapy liquid on to your palms and resume combing. She sighs again.

'He was so kind. He drank too much – it's what killed him. But he was never mean with the drink, you know?'

You wonder how she decides which vowels to inflate and which to flatten. The tat separates in your hand as you stroke the gel through it. She gives an enormous sniff, then mews with pleasure.

'Thanks so much for doing this, love. That feels really lovely. I'm heartbroken, you know? People tell me it'll get better. I just don't see how.' She shoves her hands into her eye sockets and rubs. 'I think I'll feel like this for ever.'

For the first time you notice Mary has a peculiar mound on her neck, just below her ear. It has two tiny zeniths and the slightest dip of a valley in between, like a miniature mountain range made of gelatin. You wonder if the boyfriend ever prodded the peaks of this little skin tag. You wonder if he had a nickname for it.

'They haven't chosen a headstone yet, so I took some flowers to make it look less horrible.'

The image of a chunky bouquet appears at Mary's shoulder. Pink carnations and white lilies and things that look like roses, all bundled together with pale-green cellophane.

'That bitch'll probably take them away though. You should've seen the ones on there when I visited. She has no taste.'

The only way you know how often your mother visits the cemetery is by the frequency with which she replaces the cartons of plant food. Sometimes, if she goes to bed early, you'll take the car keys from her bag and open the boot, weigh up the cartons. When one is nearly empty you bid it farewell, and, sure enough, the next time you check, it will have been replaced. You suspect your mother, exhaustively generous in spirit, feeds the plants on other graves, and you picture her lugging the heavy container from plot to plot, feeding the geraniums and lilies and carnations left for dead strangers in red football shirts.

As you get to the bottom of Mary's hair you find another enormous knot. It feels like a ball of wool, and as you try to separate individual strands they break off in your hands until your palms, sticky with gel, are covered in hairs. You grasp for the product on the counter but when you press on the nozzle there is a snapping noise. You press again and there is only a wet splutter – nothing comes out.

'You all right back there, love?' She's swiping through pictures, absent-minded. You nod, and then realize she can't see you, so you whisper, 'Yes,' and struggle to keep your voice steady. You try to plait the hair anyway, but the lump sits out to one side like an osteochondroma. You try the can again – nothing. You look around and see the container of hand soap sitting by the sink. 'Kind and healing', it says on the label. You press on the pump and the soap comes out white and gloopy. You massage it into the mass of hair. Strands slide apart and you separate them into sections, but all through the hair there is now white goo and an occasional cluster of bubbles. Mary says, 'Finished, love?' and you say, 'Not yet.'

'No rush. I love having my hair played with.' She sighs. 'He knew just how to take care of me.'

You put your hands under the tap and then your wet hands to the ends of her hair and try to wipe away the soap. The hair erupts with foam and you stare at it. The door opens and your boss walks in.

'I've just realized, man, the rota's actually in my office if you're looking for—' He stops and looks from Mary to you. 'What's going on in here, then? This isn't a rec centre, guys. Mary, haven't you got work to do?' Mary's fists clench. She gets up from the stool and turns and rolls her eyes at you. A single bubble floats through the air as her hair swings. You smile weakly. She says, 'Thanks, love,' and walks out. You and your boss stare at one another.

'What's a rec centre?'

He frowns. 'What's that?'

You look at your hands, covered in soap bubbles and hair. 'Nothing.'

He affects a jokey tone. 'Don't be coming in here to distract people, all right, man? Especially if you're not even here to work.'

You nod, and he leaves. You look at yourself in the small cracked mirror. Your face is pale and your forehead shiny. You walk to one of the shelves and take two Freddo bars out of a box. You put them in your pocket.

Andrea spots you as you emerge from the storeroom. She beckons you over. You like Andrea, and you specifically like the nature of your friendship, which seems dependent on your knowing very little about each other. She has a gravelly voice and braids held together in a ponytail and a big white smile. She's kind to you, and so you can't help imagining having sex with her. You think sex with Andrea would be nice. There would be laughter – you can picture the two of you waking up and her playing with the soft water balloons of your breasts. As you approach she smiles, and speaks under her breath.

'You get stuck in the storeroom with big sexy Mary?'

You nod.

'Was she going on about her dead, married boyfriend again?'

You nod again and she barks out a laugh. 'I know, I know, it's awful that he's dead, but I swear they went on, like, two dates. Seriously. Don't let her twist your ear about it; she loves the drama. She'll be in an ad for Scottish fucking Widows next.'

You laugh nervously.

'You OK?'

Your voice is quiet. 'I did her hair.'

'What's that?'

'Nothing.'

'You have an exam today, right?'

You nod.

'You'll kill it.' She blows you a kiss and walks away. You put your hand into your pocket and grip the stolen chocolate. You walk towards the automatic doors. Mary is behind the counter, inspecting the ends of her hair, then her fingers. She frowns. You press your chin to your chest and walk out.

When you open the car door the warmth of the interior lands on you. Your hands are sticky with melted chocolate and hair gel and soap and saliva and you scrabble to get the key into the ignition. You stare at yourself in the rear-view mirror, then close your eyes and take three deep breaths. Your exam is in 105 minutes.

You try not to think about the future. When you do, it seems to come in stock video clips that have nothing to do with what is happening in your life now. The only connection is that you are there, somehow, as if by accident.

Sometimes you see yourself as a stand-up comedian, pacing a brightly lit stage in loose-fitting trousers and white trainers, telling the punchline to a story you've never heard before. You are quick and bright and loud and after the show you go to a pub with friends and you drink beer.

You can see yourself in an office, wearing tight green trousers and a white shirt, a matching green jacket draped over the back of your chair. On the desk in front of you is a phone and a book filled with phone numbers and an open laptop with a spreadsheet on the screen. Under your desk is a pair of high heels and a pair of white trainers, although nobody minds when you walk to the office kitchenette barefoot. You wait for the kettle to boil and you read the messages printed on the mugs: *I like my coffee dark and bitter (like my soul)*; *Home is where your mum is*; *Tea Break?* While you read them a man in a pale-blue shirt with sweat patches under his arms walks in. He flirts with you, 'On the caffeine again?' and you both laugh at the arduousness of your shared duties. After work you go to a bar with your colleagues and you drink white wine.

You can see yourself in a hotel suite, squishing together two ends of a fat pillow and setting it on top of a neatly folded pyjama set. You go into the en suite and set a wrapped square of soap on the counter; you take a face cloth and wipe around the rim of the sink. Your uniform is neat and navy and close-fitting. It shows off your now-small waist. Your hair is in a high ponytail and you are wearing white trainers. You bundle together the dirty towels and drop them into the wheeled laundry basket. You hold the door open with one trainered foot and push the trolley out into the hall. After work you go to a restaurant. You arrive early so you can change out of your uniform in the toilets and when you emerge there is a man sitting at a table, waiting. He stands up and kisses you. You drink the gin and tonic he has ordered for you.

These images exist as clearly, and seem as probable, if not

more so, as your life currently. None of them are any more or any less appealing than the others, and what matters is that in all of them you seem content and things are decided. The difficulty lies in the great grey expanse between the you of now and the you of these images. The necessary steps towards one are so different from those towards another that it seems reckless to choose. Instead, you float closer and closer to the edge of that expanse, not allowing yourself to think about what will happen when you reach it. You're not convinced you won't just fade into nothing, into grey dust. This outcome, too, seems like something beyond your control.

You drive slowly, your eyes moving from the twisty uphill roads to the flickering dashboard clock. In the dense, oppressive heat of the car your smell seems to mix with that of the warm upholstery. It reminds you of the inside of a pet shop – moist and stale. It smells like pellets and fur and shit. You turn the dial of the air conditioning up and point the fan at your face until your eyes prickle and the hairs on your arms stand on end. The small blue pillow hanging from the mirror sways back and forth.

The skin on the backs of your hands starts to itch from the cold air. Not aware you are going to do it until you do, you turn the car suddenly and violently into a narrow side street. The car rocks to one side and a prolonged honk comes from behind you. Without slowing you pull the car up on to the kerb and then brake. The tyres squeal and everything leans forward for a moment before jerking back. You grip the steering wheel, breathing heavily. You get out of the car.

The pub at the top of the street has been a Wetherspoons for as long as you can remember, but the old wooden sign is still outside; it has a silhouette of deer on a hill. You remember a conversation between two hedgehogs, from a cartoon you watched when you were little:

'I wonder what White Deer Park looks like.'

'Lots of white deer, I suppose.'

It was here that you met Donal, the beautiful musician with the Cheestring legs for the first time. It was also here that you met him for drinks a week after. Three weeks from now, when exam season is over, the students in your year will come here for cheap shots of tequila and vodka with lemonade. You will be eighteen by then. Everyone will wear their school shirts, newly ruined with felt-tip signatures and crude drawings. The beautiful girls will wear their shirts knotted just below their breasts; the popular boys will have their ties tied around their heads. The thought of going makes you anxious. The thought of not going makes you anxious.

The pub's smoking area is shaded and moody-looking, with empty barrels flung across it as decor. Most of the tables are empty, although one has an elderly man reading a newspaper, and another a middle-aged couple, sitting across from one another. As you stand in the doorway you wish you'd taken your blazer off – it feels heavy across your shoulders. You listen to the laughter of the middle-aged couple, too raucous and joyful, like teenagers in an ad for skincare products. You watch them.

You know your father from the back, from years spent staring at his head from the back seat of the car. You know the thinning brown-grey hair that forms an earthy Catherine wheel; at its centre a patch of numinous scalp. He's wearing a striped shirt and the flesh of his neck blurs the edge of the collar. Sitting opposite him is a woman. She has glossy black hair in a bob and its colour is too stark against the smoking area's soft lighting. Every hair looks like it has been individually lacquered and the result is disconcerting, like a CGI simulation of hair. She is wearing dark-purple lipstick. It has bled into the rivulets around her mouth and, unlike her hair, her mouth is slightly out of focus, like two slug-shaped bruises meeting at either end. When she smiles you can see that one of her front teeth is dark with a smudge of purple, and you can imagine pressing a finger against it and feeling the tooth give under the pressure. You stand at the edge of the smoking area for a while, watching them, before inching over to the closest picnic table. You lower yourself on to a bench. You lift your legs over the beam and slide them under the table, keeping your eyes fixed on the woman.

She's wearing a sleeveless dress. You follow the line of her arm, from the bare shoulder down the upper arm – it has a pronounced curve of muscle – to the elbow resting on the wooden table to the forearm to the chunky gold bangle on the wrist to the back of the hand. You think you can almost make out the fraying constellation of lentigines when she scratches her nose. When she lowers her hand she coils her fingers up with your father's. You put your hand in your pocket and crunch the foil of the silver pill packet between your fingers, the packet with only one blue, diamond-shaped pill remaining.

You picture it. You picture the woman nervously adjusting the plum dust ruffle on her bed, anticipating his arrival. You picture him standing outside. He checks his reflection in the brass doorbell before pressing it – he's been looking forward to this for days. You picture her giggling as he presents a bottle of red wine and kisses her cheek. You hear the wet slur of their words as their teeth get blacker and their eyes get redder. You picture your father fumbling in the bathroom with the foil packet, popping one of the diamonds out from its see-through bubble. You picture him swallowing it, wedging his head under the tap, straightening up, performing a jumpy dance while he waits. He smiles as he feels the pill smooth the creases in the fabric of his cock, feels it rise jerkily like the arm of a crane. You picture him looming over the woman with the glossy hair, filling her up and steering her, her blurry lips parted and the black arches of her gums and the smudge on her tooth exposed. You hear their breathing as they lie side by side on the rumpled bed sheets afterwards, the lights dimmed.

You want so desperately to make it ugly, but it isn't. You picture him lifting one arm and you picture her rolling towards him and you picture him holding her for as long as possible before he has to go. You picture him leaving, the apology in his smile, the sadness in hers. You picture her returning to the bathroom to make eye contact with herself. She slides in the plastic retainer that lives on the edge of the sink and makes her feel like a teenager.

You know now that this is what your father does. When you call him and he doesn't answer or when he comes in late on a Friday night and shakes the ill-fitting wooden doors in their frames; when he's sitting at the kitchen table staring blankly at the crack in the wall, his mouth ajar, it is because of this woman. This normal-looking woman is the reason your father has cause to smile at nothing, when nothing has been said. What reason would he have otherwise, to smile? This woman with the glossy hair in the sleeveless dress is laughing at something he has said. When was the last time he made a woman laugh?

The woman has stood up from the table. You see her mouth move around the words 'ladies' room', and you wonder if it is important to her that your father doesn't think of her sitting on a toilet seat with her thighs spread and her dress in folds around her middle. As her arms press themselves to her sides teardrop-shaped pillows of flesh appear at her armpits. You have the same droplets when you wear sleeveless tops. You always try to press them inwards so they stay concealed. This requires rigorous attention so instead you have decided not to wear sleeveless tops at all. That this woman has the same problem and has chosen to either not care or to conceal her discomfort fills you with a mixture of warmth and pity. A moment later it occurs to you that perhaps she doesn't view the teardrop folds of fat under her arms as a problem at all, as something that needs to be solved, and this fills you with a different feeling.

She circles the table. As she passes your father she puts her hand on his shoulder and kisses the top of his head, right on the spot where he has a raised, tan mole, and you feel the jerk of nausea in your throat. She crosses the smoking area, her heels clacking on the paving stones. She is swallowed by the pub and your father puts his hand to his back pocket and slides out his phone. You sit, inert, and wish you had tried to call him earlier, so that he could see your name on the screen now and feel guilty.

You keep your hand firm on the pill packet and wonder if your father can sense its closeness. You run your thumb over the popped domes on the blister pack. You finger it faster and faster, until you're amazed the others in the garden can't hear the metallic crackle. What you are feeling, more than anything else, is something like relief.

You wonder sometimes if your parents feel cheated; if they feel like they traded in their happiness for a daughter who has yielded little. You imagine it's much easier to endure unhappiness if you have a child who is beautiful and clever and loved. What have you been worth? You like that your father might have realized this. You like that his actions might negate the need for you to be something better than what you are. You find yourself jealous for a moment; jealous of your father, jealous of the woman, jealous of the old man sitting at the other table, reading the newspaper.

You wonder what would happen if the woman came back from the bathroom to find you sitting in her seat, opposite your father. You wonder what your father would say if you walked to their table, sat down, said, 'Hi, Dad.' You wonder what you would say if she lied to you, if she said, 'I'm a friend of your father's.'

Your fists are pressed tightly into your thighs. Your chest feels warm and tight and your breathing feels ragged, like your lungs are bags of crisps left for months at the bottom of a school bag. You press the heels of your hands into the concaves of your eye sockets.

Without allowing yourself time to wonder what you ought to do, you are suddenly performing a slow and ungainly leg lift over the bench. Your tights snag on a barb of wood and a ladder appears above your knee. You make a point of smiling, to make it obvious to anyone looking that you are not bothered by your own clumsiness. You walk into the pub, keeping your head down and your arms folded protectively across your chest in case your father looks up from his phone. The abrupt darkness of being inside makes you put an arm to the wall to steady yourself, and you wait for your eyes to adjust to the gloom. You head towards the toilets, towards the woman in the kitten heels and the sleeveless dress. Your feet make clattering sounds on the wooden floor, and you try to keep your steps as light as possible, holding all your body weight in your knees.

The pub's toilet doors are painted, with translucent panes of glass and novelty signs to demarcate the men's and women's. With the door still partially open behind you, you find the woman. You collide with her. The ball of her foot, squeezed into the flat triangle of one canvas kitten heel, presses down on your toes. Spots appear in front of your eyes and your foot combusts with pain. Ripples vibrate up your leg. You gasp, and she steps back.

'Oh, God! I'm so sorry, pet!'

You can feel your eyes bulging at her. You don't say anything; you're concentrating on not crumpling to the floor and nursing your foot in your lap like a swaddled orphan. You stay still. The woman looks at you and her blurry mouth tightens in concern.

'Oh, pet, I'm really sorry. I didn't even see you there. Are you OK?'

You nod and she takes a step forward. For one awful moment you think she is going to hug you and you put your hands in front of you in a warning gesture. She takes a step to the side and you realize she is just trying to leave. You don't move.

'I am really, really sorry. Sorry – would you mind if I just . . .'

She leaves the sentence unfinished, and it occurs to you that she and your father are very well suited. You contemplate not moving, making her stay in here with you. You wonder about making this woman confront the image of your exploded toenail. She raises her eyebrows at you, confused. You step to one side and she gives you an anxious smile and then leaves. It's clear she doesn't know who you are – your father has either never mentioned you or has never shown her a photo.

There are thirteen photos in the photo gallery on your father's phone; you feature in three of them. The passcode to your father's phone is 0206333. He doesn't know you know this.

Your eyes adjust more quickly this time to the dark of the bar. You find a patch of bare wall by the door that looks out into the smoking area. With your body leaning against it, turned towards the pub's interior, you twist your head around until the muscles in your neck protest. You watch your father and the woman, sitting at the table.

You wonder how long it took her to get ready for this midday drink with your father at the pub. You wonder if he tells her often that she looks good, if he uses the word 'beautiful'. You wonder if they both know that 'beautiful' means something different as you get older or lonelier. Maybe he says 'lovely', instead. Anything can be lovely: a milk jug on a rustic tablecloth; a prize-winning horse; a formidable, gnarled tree. You wonder if she tells him he looks handsome, which is an even more confusing word to navigate.

Women with strong noses can be handsome. So too, probably, can old pieces of furniture.

Your father is gripping a pint of something amber-coloured. She has a glass of white wine. You lurk in the cool dark of the pub's narthex – there is nothing in here except you and an empty umbrella stand and a yellow plastic Labrador with a slot in its head. 'Donate to Guide Dogs UK', the red tag on its collar says. 'What a stupid name for a dog,' you mutter. Your quiet laughter sounds deranged.

'And then he had me backdate everything he's done for the last six weeks, even though we both know rightly he's not going to have to show it to anyone. I feel like he's deliberately picking on me.'

She has an accent you can't locate. She says 'me' like *meh*. You roll 'backdate' around your mouth – from her it comes out like *backdeh*. You note your father's big hand on top of hers. You note the way he's looking intently at her. You wonder if this is part of their acquiescence; that they pretend to find one another interesting.

'You're too good for that place. They don't deserve you.'

She likes this; she shakes her head slightly and smiles. You look for a teleprompter at the far end of the garden, feeding your father lines. He says it again, with renewed vigour: 'You are. You're too good for that place.' You wonder when he learned to start saying the right things. You wonder if he always knew, but just didn't want any sort of accord with your mother. You think your mother could have been happier if someone had just acknowledged she was too good for her surroundings.

'I just – I mean, when my mother died I took five days

off. Five! And he's never even acknowledged it! No, "Oh, thanks, Janine, for not letting the whole place fall into disreputance!" Honestly, he's got it in for me.'

You wonder if your father notices her grammatical errors or the way she leaves the 't' off certain words. You wonder if it bothers him. Your mother is smart, smarter than him, smarter than you. You think it is this surplus of intelligence that makes her so furious and anxious and dissatisfied. Perhaps your father is relieved to be around someone different — perhaps he fetishizes her mistakes. You wonder how her mother died; if there were ham sandwiches at the funeral; if there was an open coffin. You wonder if she exaggerates the situation with the man at work because she thinks your father will like it.

Your father is leaning over the table. It takes you a moment to realize he is going to kiss her. As his head and broad back and wide hips obscure her entirely from view you drift back into the bar.

'What can I get you?'

The barman is something between muscular and fat. His neck is broad and his face is friendly. You look to see if he has prominent bones in his shoulders and you are relieved that he doesn't. You order four double vodkas and lemonade.

'Four?'

'My friends are coming to meet me.'

'Did you have an exam this morning?'

You tell him yes, and when he asks how it went you say you are just relieved that it is over and that your friends are coming to meet you and that soon it will be summer and you will be able to celebrate. The lemonade comes out of a mechanical hose. It looks like something that ought to be protruding from a monster, storming a city.

'Need a hand with those?'

You tell him no, that you can manage, that your friends had better get here soon before you drink them all, and at this he laughs and says, 'Be good.'

You drink the first vodka and lemonade quickly, forgetting to stir it with the straw. When you reach the bottom of the glass the taste is suddenly harsh and chemical and your stomach lurches violently. If you lean forward in your seat you can just see out the open door, into the garden. When your father comes in to buy more drinks you peek around the corner of the booth and watch him at the bar. You hold your mouth slightly open, hoping the air will clean the unwelcome vodka residue off your tongue. Your father sways back and forth from the balls of his feet to his heels.

'You've caught the sun a bit there, big man.'

The barman gestures at your father's head. Your father laughs good-naturedly. He puts his fingers to his burned scalp.

'Oh! Aye – guess I should get a hat or something. A nice headscarf, maybe!'

Both men laugh at the idea of him wearing a floral headscarf. Your father orders a beer and a white wine.

'So the lovely lady's the Thelma to your Louise then?' the barman asks as he unscrews a bottle cap. It takes your father a moment to get the joke. When he does he laughs loudly.

'Hopefully with a bit more of an auspicious ending!' he says.

The barman chuckles and holds a pint glass up to one of the taps. 'There you go, mate,' he says and slides the drinks over. Your father pays and walks out. You watch him ease his thick legs in their beige trousers over the wooden bench. You see him putting his hand to his head, talking excitedly. You see the woman laughing. You wonder if it's genuine.

You remember to stir the second vodka and lemonade, put your lips around the straw and suck it down fast. Already your thoughts are dislodging in your head. You picture your father and Janine in a convertible, both wearing cat's-eye sunglasses. There's a canyon, a police chase, a fade-out to credits. You've only seen parodies of the film, never the real thing.

Janine's laughter finds its way in from outside. You get started on the third drink.

Leaning over the toilet bowl, the miasma of bleach and piss makes your eyes water. You hear a gulp sound come from somewhere deep inside you and then you taste acid. You vomit up all the day's nauseas. The vomit is pure fluid, a poisonous citrus colour that pales and darkens as the jet stream squeezes itself out of you. Once finished, you slump against the stall door, your legs spread wide on the floor. Your stomach feels vacuum-sealed. There is a dull pain in your chest and your brain feels sore and the bones around your eyes ache.

You used to get sick a lot, when you were little – always in the middle of the night. You would wake to find a pool of salty, stagnant water under your tongue and a tugging sensation in your stomach. By the time you were on your knees, heaving into the toilet bowl, your mother was already there, loosening the hair stuck to your forehead and rubbing your back with a purposeful, circular motion. When she was sure you were finished she would get you a glass of water and if you were really upset she wouldn't insist that you brush your teeth. She would sit with you in your bedroom, the only light coming from the bathroom across the landing. She would go back and clean up after you had gone to sleep.

When you were fifteen you caught norovirus. It was three consecutive nights of your mother kneeling on the bathmat next to you. On the first night she didn't say much – she lined up glasses of water on the windowsill. On the second night she joked, 'When you have a child of your own you can let me know how you get on with night-time vomit duty.' On the third night she joked, 'It'll be my lucky day when your boyfriend takes over night-time vomit duty.' At the time this imaginary future child and future boyfriend had seemed not just appealing prospects, but perfectly attainable ones.

You stand up and flush the toilet. There are still orange splatters on the cistern and on the seat and along the rim of the bowl. You unlock the cubicle door.

'Are you all right?'

The woman is tall. She has short, brassy-coloured hair and purple-rimmed glasses. She's wearing a diaphanous cream top covered in blue paisley swirls. It has an elastic hem stretched tight around her hips. She looks at you with a mixture of suspicion and concern. You open your mouth and hear a voice like yours, only more languid, reply.

'I'm fine, but I think someone's been sick in there. It's disgusting.'

She looks to the cubicle, then back to you. You turn and leave the bathroom.

There is something lying by the side of the road. It looks clean and plump and fluffy, like a new feather duster, and you briefly entertain leaning over and wiping your hands on it, to try to get rid of the lingering odour of vomit and cheap hand soap. When you get closer you realize it's a dead kitten. Its legs are curled into its torso and its head is pressed to its chest. It looks like an asterisk and a closed parenthesis; a bass clef; the curved end of a hockey stick. You get down on your haunches and touch the velvety pink ovals and circles on the base of its paws. The body is still warm. You wonder what you're supposed to do. You can't take it to the vet – the kitten would be taken from you and burned with all the other dead animals. It would become run-off at the bottom of an incinerator – little chunks of charcoal and handfuls of dust.

You hear the slow rumble of a car in the distance. The streets here are riddled with curves and speed bumps – you're surprised a car could even gain enough speed to kill a cat, but then, it's small. The bones in its neck are probably about as breakable as the seam in a KitKat. The sound of the car is getting louder, though you still can't see it. You pull the fabric of your jumper out from your body with one hand and scoop the kitten into it with the other. You walk quickly. The car approaches from behind and moves past – you make eye contact first with the driver and then with the child in the back. You wonder if you shook the kitten would all the fragments of broken bone inside clatter against one another, like a drawstring bag full of baby teeth.

★

When you finally find yourself next to the black Toyota you are out of breath. You open the passenger door and place the kitten on the seat. You pull your jumper over your head – the fabric in the armpits is darker, with two matching crescents of sweat – and lay it over the kitten so only its face is visible. The car is parked at a tilt, two wheels on the kerb, two off, and you stand with your head at the same angle for a moment. With your head still leaning you look around. The terraced houses are now capsizing on their foundations; a man pushes his lawnmower sideways along the steep incline of his garden. The mower motor rumbles. The dust of dead grass floats in the air.

The car's interior has cooled. The atmosphere inside seems tactile and misty, like the air in front of a supermarket fridge. As you turn the key in the ignition you set your other hand down on the kitten and stroke it through the jumper. You keep your hand on top of its abdomen as you steer the car, one-handed, off the kerb. It thumps on to the flat road. You turn on the radio and the volume is set so loud that the strident blare of it makes you recoil and pull your foot off the clutch. Time concertinas for a moment, stretching and halting. The car leaps forward, you bounce in your seat, the dashboard flashes, a bell chimes, the music cuts out.

You sit very still, breathing heavily. You restart the engine. The music shouts at you again and you pull your hand away from the kitten and grasp the volume dial, twisting it until the music sits on top of the muffled buzz of the lawnmower, which now glides easily over a once-more flat earth. You ease the car down the street, leaning forward, your knuckles prominent and white as you grip the steering wheel. The houses float by and you struggle to remember if they were always terraced or if they have melted together in your waterlogged sight.

The front left tyre slumps into a pothole and your whole body seems to fall with it. You watch your knuckles, the thin red lines that have appeared in your skin as it gets stretched over bone. Your right foot, with its big toe wrapped in its turban of bandages, feels numb. You apply too much then too little then too much pressure on the throttle. The car goes quick then slow then quick, bumping along the quiet street. You stare out at the occasional residents. You see a young woman on a green plastic chair. Her trousers are in rolls around her knees and the straps of her sun top are pushed down so they droop over her upper arms. You see another woman at an open upstairs window, pulling clumps of hair out of a hairbrush. Another man is carrying a terracotta planter filled with nursery plants, young and tender with their buds squeezed shut. He staggers after a woman with leathery skin, who meanders back and forth in front of the house. You allow their movements to dictate the opening and closing of your eyes. Your eyelids get abandoned at half mast and you handle the steering wheel clumsily. Your history exam is in fourteen minutes.

The street bleeds out on to a roundabout. The cars going past all seem to be the same colours and so the roundabout looks like a carousel or a tornado – each car trapped in the centrifuge.

You watch them whizz past. You take one hand off the

steering wheel and stroke the ear of the kitten with one finger. Its fur feels thin and spare and barely able to cover the coldness underneath. A gap is approaching between the cars, an empty plot on the carousel platform's gilt surface.

You ease your foot down on the accelerator. The gap is here. You lean forward in the expectation of movement and when nothing happens you look at your feet. You struggle to feel the pedal. You press down, hard. The engine revs and the car zips forward, too fast. The roundabout approaches rapidly. You move your foot to the brake and the car stops. You look to your right. Cars are coming. You are planted in the middle of the lanes, perpendicular to oncoming traffic. The cars coming are silver and silver and blue. You press down hard on the pedal and the revving engine yells at you. You push down the handbrake. The small body of the car darts forward. It mounts the kerb of the roundabout and keeps going. You assume the brace position. You pull your knees to your chest, both feet now hovering above the pedals. Something in the engine flutters like a palpitating heart. The car does three hops forward.

thump thump thump

You tug at the handbrake and everything halts and your head smacks against the window. The car becomes violently still.

The dashboard flashes and a bell chimes.

You close your eyes.

Seventeen years old – April 14th (one month ago)

You are drunk. The fake, curated graffiti on the hostel bar wall is inflating and deflating, and your voice is simultaneously too loud and muffled, like it's coming from inside an airing cupboard. The barman – *Yahcob* – is gripping your hand and leading you down a flight of stairs. The floor is black and speckled and sticky, and you realize that this is the nightclub, and you are excited that you'll be able to tell the girls that you made it here when they didn't. There are groups of people sprinkled across the dance floor. The barman's hand stays on yours and he leads you to a corner. You put your palms on his shoulders and find the hard knuckle of bone. You press your fingers into it and imagine twiddling it like a dial on a console. His smile meets your mouth and his hands find the soft dollop of flesh above your waistband, strategically concealed beneath your top.

And now he's taking you somewhere else. You feel the soles of your shoes peeling off the floor with every step and suddenly you're in bright white, like when an optician turns the lights on after an examination. You put your hand to your eyes and stumble into the wall and the wall is white, the surface of it is gritty with dust and the barman is in front of you, pushing you against the wall and kissing you. You put your hands in his hair. He puts his hands between your legs. He starts to rub, and it doesn't really feel like anything, but you let him keep doing it and

and now he has turned you around so you're facing the wall and you notice there is a long, thin, black crack in the white dust and

and he's tugging at your jeans, tugging them down over the parts of your middle that undulate like a waterbed and you wonder if the fabric has left an angry red indent in your skin. You try to speak but your tongue feels heavy and

and he's pulling the jeans down round your knees and you place your hands against the salty grit of the wall and try to push yourself away from it but then his hand is on the back of your head and he's pressing your face into the wall and you feel the rough texture rubbing at your forehead like sandpaper and you say, 'No, no,'
　　you think
　　you think you hear your voice saying 'no', but nothing happens, so maybe you didn't say anything. His hand is wrapped up in your hair and your eyes are level with the thin black line.

You try again, 'No,' and this time the voice coming out of you sounds like your mother's: it's deeper and older than yours. You wonder when she got here, and won't she be angry at the thick, red ridge in your skin – she's always telling you not to buy clothes a size too small. She speaks again, 'No, no,' and this time you definitely hear her, but his hand is still pressing your head while his other hand is somewhere at your waist and your mother will be angry that he isn't listening to her.

You squint your eyelids so they match the thin black line. You imagine yourself inside it, inside the crack in the wall that is so thin and so small and if you were inside it you would be just one small part of one small unit of blackness. You are about to disappear inside it entirely when

when the pressure comes, and it's hard and it's wrong and it's painful but not like the first time — it's in the wrong place, the wrong hole. The pressure comes like the end of a rolling pin, like a closed fist. It stretches you and rips you. You hear someone speaking, and it's your voice and it isn't, it's younger and wet and sad and it's saying, 'No, no, no,' and you push yourself away from the wall and you twist around and

and then you're in the dark corridors of the hostel, stumbling. Your jeans aren't pulled far enough up for you to fasten them so the fly gapes. You're trying to run but it's more like a waddle, like you've been sitting down for too long and everything is stiff and tender and

and then you're in the bathroom. You're sitting on the toilet with your jeans pulled down around your knees. You're staring into them, at the large, rust-coloured stain – the colour of blood, the colour of shit. You feel torn. Your tears are salty and there are loud, gasping heaves coming from your throat as you rock back and forth. Your head sloshes with bubblegum mouthwash and whisky. Your eyes feel like they've been popped out and washed in bleach and put back in your head and

and then you're in bed. You're curled up on the white sheet, still wearing your jeans. The girls are asleep in the beds around you and the floor is covered in McDonald's detritus: squashed burger boxes and a couple of sagging, errant chips and a receipt scrunched in a ball. The smell is that comforting, fake-meat smell, warm and salty and Styrofoamy. You close your eyes and feel the plunge again, the split. You open your eyes and the world spins like kebab meat and you realize that it's you who's spinning, that you now orbit the hole that has been left in you. You want to reach your hands into the dark and catch all the bits that are leaking out. You want to shove them back inside you but it's late and you're tired and every part of you aches and

and then you're on a train platform, hugging yourself, trying to hold all the parts of you together. You're still in the same clothes and you wonder if the girls can smell what has happened. You struggle to stop yourself thinking about it; you quiver with the aftershocks of it; the breath seizes in your throat. On the train you press your eyes to the window and angle yourself in your chair so nobody can see your face, and when a woman with a nametag asks if she can see your ticket and if you are having a nice day no words come out. You stare at her. You don't say anything.

Seventeen years old – May 16th (today)

You open your eyes and everything is blurry. The dashboard is flashing red and orange with warning signs.

You push the car door open and unclick your seat belt

and crawl on to the grass. The bones in your face seem loose. You cross your legs and walk your fingers up the ladder in your tights. Your skull feels like a sandwich bag full of water. You tilt your head and feel the water pool in one side. You tilt it the other way and feel the other ear and cheek fill out.

Cars continue to go past on the roundabout. Some slow and you can see the drivers craning their necks to get a glimpse of you, sitting on the grass, your hands by your sides.

You picture the other students, sitting in rows and columns like the grids on a French window. Rachael will have a Bic biro gripped in her hand and three spare Bic biros on the desk in front of her. The school desks are old and worn and the wood is defaced with years of pen scratches from years of students. Rachael will probably spend the few minutes before the exam reading the words etched on to her desk: 'G&A 2012'; 'Chris was here!!'; 'Fuck the police'. You wonder if she ever glanced back to look for you, if she wondered where you were.

The sun rolls out from behind a cloud and begins to sizzle the fine hairs on the top of your head. You lie back. Your eyes close.

Your most vivid memory of your uncle is this: an evening spent at his house several months before he died. Your mother and father sat in the kitchen, drinking cider he'd brought back from France. There was music playing. As was customary, you soon lost interest in the adults and wanted to play online solitaire on his laptop. In your rush to open the game, you closed a work document without saving it. He was kind about it, but strained, and whenever you think about him it amazes you that he was capable of kindness and patience amidst the interminable soundtrack of his fear. The day of the funeral, it occurred to you that you would never get the chance to make it up to him.

The health centre does not look like a health centre. It has a porch, a wooden front door with panels, a car park that is little more than a large driveway. You stand on the other side of the street and watch it, picking bits of roundabout grass out of your hair. A woman emerges with a toddler and a baby. The toddler rejects the coat held out to her. The baby wrestles in his pram, screams. The woman looks tired. She takes out her phone and calls a taxi, shouts 'Sorry? What was that? Sorry?' over the baby's wails and the toddler's yells. Your eyes feel dried-out and powdery, like two waxy teardrops on a hyacinth, and you close them for a moment.

You wonder at what point a mother's love gets exhausted. You think about your mother, wiping blood from your head with a tissue. You wonder if she ever wishes she could start over with a new, clean baby. 'I know that you can be great,' she'd said. You wonder what she'd say now. The taxi comes and the woman wobbles the pram towards it, holding the toddler's coat in one hand. The toddler drops something, but nobody notices, and when the taxi pulls away you cross the street and pick it up. It's a small, yellow, plastic saddle, belonging to a toy horse. You put it back on the ground.

You often think about orphans. You sometimes wish that you were one; that your parents had died when you were tiny and half formed. You wonder if it might be easier to grow up with the event already behind you; like surgery in childhood to repair a cleft palate. This seems preferable to the alternative; that your parents' death still awaits you. Can you become an orphan in adulthood? Or is it something that has to develop when you're young, like a port-wine stain or bone density? You look at the people walking around you – how many of them have already lost their parents? The woman sitting outside the pub in the sleeveless dress – her mother is dead and she only took five days off work. You wonder at how people can continue to breathe and walk and exist after their loved ones become irretrievable.

You push the door open. The receptionist looks up at you, smiles. You follow the sign to the walk-in sexual health clinic.

Your uncle used to say you would grow up to look like your mother. 'She's going to be a tiny, fairy thing, like you, Squishy.' Then he'd cut you another slice of rich-tasting European fruit bread and say, 'Unless I have anything to do with it.' You suspect another advantage of having your parents die young is they never have to know how you turned out.

The waiting room has four people in it: a man with a beard and tight jeans; a woman in a grey skirt suit with her dark hair in a ponytail; a woman in navy tracksuit bottoms; a girl in the same uniform as you, though you don't recognize her. You sit down and the chair rattles – one leg is shorter than the other three. The woman in the tracksuit bottoms is sitting on a dark-blue sofa. Her legs are spread open to the room. Her mouth opens with every chew of her gum and you can see the white columns forming and collapsing as the gum is stretched between her upper and lower molars. Every so often her chewing happens in time with the clunk of the second hand on the clock.

All four are looking at their phones – the woman in the grey skirt suit's brow is furrowed with the intensity of her looking. Occasionally a nurse or doctor strides through and they hide their phones between their legs, as though scared of being reprimanded.

On the wall opposite you there's a poster. It's red and instead of the letter I there's an exclamation mark between the H and the V. No matter which way you look the redness of the poster encroaches on your vision. You lean back in your chair, and with your head facing forward you angle your eyes to the left and look at the phone screen of the woman with the chewing gum. She's scrolling back and forth between three pictures, and the rough edge of her unevenly bitten thumbnail taps against the glass. In one picture she's naked in front of a mirror and the photo is of her reflection. Her hip is cocked at an extreme angle and you can see the bare beige triangle of her mons pubis. With her free hand she's squeezing one of her breasts and her lips are parted. In the second picture she's lying down, still naked, her upper half propped up on a pillow. She's holding the camera above herself and you can see nothing below her waist. In the third there's just a pair of legs, spread wide. The beige triangle is pointed upwards, into the air. A forearm appears from the bottom of the shot and snakes up the stomach; one finger disappears over the top of the triangle.

She stops at the third picture. She zooms in on the hand draped over the bare mound between her legs, and the finger that disappears over its peak. She zooms out, but doesn't scroll back to the other pictures. It takes you a moment to realize she's stopped chewing. You glance up, and she's looking at you. Her expression is bored, non-curious.

'All right?'

Her cheek is covered in red, scabby circles, some of which interlock with others to form Venn diagrams. She puts a hand to her cheek and scratches and a cluster of skin flakes drifts downwards. Her voice breaks the glassy silence of the waiting room, and the other people jump slightly at the intrusion. You think about getting up and leaving. Instead, you nod.

'You just having a look, yeah?'

The other three have gone back to their phones, but occasionally the girl in the uniform looks up with interest. You feel your face go red. You nod again.

'Help me choose one.'

She tilts the phone towards you and you stare at the soft, bald pyramid of her crotch. She swipes and you stare at her large breasts. She swipes again and you stare at her upright, naked body, her breasts more pendulous now that she's vertical. She flicks between the photos a few times, then looks up at you again.

'Well?'

You reach over and slide your finger across the greasy glass until the photo on screen is that of the anonymous crotch, being teased with a single finger.

'Yeah, that's the one I thought as well.'

She taps the screen a few times and sends the photo to an unsaved number. She resumes chewing. You wonder if the others in the room think you are friends. A nurse appears, says, 'Kathryn?' and the woman looks up from her phone and nods. There is one loose diamond of red skin poking out from her cheek, and you wonder, given what has just happened, if it would be permissible for you to reach over and pull it off. Kathryn stands up and there is a crescent of exposed skin between the waistband of her tracksuit bottoms and the hem of her t-shirt. You can see the beginnings of the vertical cleft between her ass cheeks and the same red rings scattered across the expanse of her lower back. You want to trace them with your fingers, like patterns on a carpet. She pulls up her bottoms and follows the nurse. She turns back to you and says, 'Thanks for the help, perv,' and then winks. As she walks out of the waiting room the woman in the grey skirt suit watches her, one hand placed protectively over her stomach.

'Hi there, have you signed in?'

You jerk in your seat and your back twinges. There is a woman standing at your elbow. She's short, barely taller than you sitting down. She has glasses on a silver chain around her neck. You shake your head.

'First time here?'

You nod.

'Well, normally patients write their name and what they're here for on a slip of paper in that office.' She nods towards a door. It has a paper sign with 'Check in Here' written on it. Someone has drawn a flower with big looping petals in the corner of the sheet. 'But since you're new, I can take you through and we can have a chat, OK?'

The others watch you leave, impassive. You wonder, if this small woman were to plunge a pair of scissors into your chest, would they even react? As you follow her into the corridor you are ashamed at how much taller you are. You feel that, as a large person, you ought to seem more in control of your movements – to compensate for your obtrusive size with poise. You stumble after her, past another red sign with the capital H and the exclamation mark and the capital V. She leads you into a room with a chair and a desk and a bed on wheels with a light-grey iron frame. There is a pale-green curtain hanging from the ceiling, a set of scales on the floor. She closes the door behind you and you turn back, helpless. She gestures to the chair, and her glasses swing outwards and then bounce back on the polite swells of her cleavage.

'Just take a seat there.'

The chair slides back and thumps against the wall.

'Now, why don't you tell me what's going on?'

The woman's eyes are small and the irises nearly as dark as her pupils. She has high cheekbones and a slim nose. You realize it was odd for you to assume she was young just because she is small. Her hands are clasped on the desk in front of her, and on one finger there's a ring: gold, with two separate strands woven together. You wonder if it is an heirloom. You want to ask if her parents are dead and you want to tell her what happened in the hostel storeroom. You want to tell her about the hole inside you. You want her to laugh and tell you that you're absolutely fine. You want her to tell you that it's OK that you've been scared but that it's all going to be fine. You don't say anything.

'Are you OK? Has something happened? Whatever it is, I'm sure we can sort it.'

What if she told you something else? You think of the exclamation mark on the red poster.

You look down at the ladder in your tights and the yellow and orange splashes of vomit on your skirt. You were probably flagged up as peculiar the moment you walked in, someone to be handled delicately.

You go to stand but only make it a few inches above the chair before you fall back and it rattles against the wall again. She unclasps her hands and says, hesitant, 'Careful, now.' You try again and this time you manage it. You begin to roll your tights down. You stare fixedly at the pale-green curtain. The woman's voice is alarmed this time. 'Now there's no need to . . .' but you keep rolling until your foot is out of your tights. The floor is silver and flecked through with black. You wonder if she's ever realized the floor is made from the colours in her hair. You unwind the bandage on your toe. She puts her glasses on and bends over and looks at it. You look at the top of her head.

'Oh dear. That's quite a severe infection you have on that toenail.'

There is dried blood crusted on the skin and a flattened dollop of yellow spread over the nail's surface like buttercream. The smell of it rises up. It's egg and sulphur and musty laundry.

'Have you had this examined by anyone?'

Behind the lenses of her glasses her eyes look magnified, and the pupils and irises even darker, like drilled holes. You shake your head. Her lips are downturned in an arch and it makes the skin on her chin pucker. You want her to say that she knows there's something else going on. You want her to know without you having to tell her. You shake your head.

'OK, what you need to do is book an appointment with a podiatrist – I can get you the name and number.'

She swivels in her chair towards the computer. You slide your foot back into the leg of your tights. When you push your foot into your shoe you flinch. You turn to her and stretch your lips over your teeth. You stand up and she turns and says, 'Are you sure you're all right? Is there someone I can call for you?' You shake your head. Her kindness sits densely in the room.

You hear yourself say, 'I'm just going to use the toilet,' and you hear her say, 'Don't forget to come back for this phone number, and we can have another chat. This is examination room 11.' You hear yourself say, 'Thank you for seeing me,' and you hear her say, 'Wait, are you sure there's not—' but this conversation is now behind you. You pull the door closed and float along the corridors, past the signs to the various clinics, out the door that seems like just a regular door.

You pass a florist; a radio inside is playing 'Riders on the Storm'. The sun lowers itself in the sky behind you, and your shadow is long and thin. You spread the fingers on your left hand and watch their black, stretched fronds wiggle on the paving stones. Your breathing is heavy, and in the distance a clock chimes. You slope in the direction of home. You have zero minutes. You have zero minutes.

The sky is turning peach as you approach your street. You don't know what time it is. In the driveway of a large, detached house two adults are unloading wicker furniture from the back of a khaki Land Rover. A small girl sits, legs crossed, in a chair abandoned next to it. When she curls her legs towards her chest you can see the herringbone pattern of the wicker canes embedded in the underside of her thighs.

She's holding a carton of Ribena, and purple water drips from the straw and is filtered through the holes in the chair and on to the tarmac. She stares at you, and the strength of her look alerts the attention of her parents, who stop what they're doing and look at you too. You wander on.

When you reach the last of the larger detached houses, you stop. It is an exposed red-brick cube with an overgrown lawn dotted with dandelions and a broken letterbox – the slat hangs off its hinge. The white front door is dirty, and it's as though the smaller, scruffier neighbourhood where you live has begun to infect it. You sit down on the kerb and spread your legs wide. The road is empty, and a few moments later you hear a thud as the Land Rover doors are slammed shut. You feel in your pocket and pull out the slab of porridge wrapped in kitchen roll. You set it beside you and a small bird arrives, commences pecking. The bird is brown, with an orange beak and eyes like black marbles. When you reach out it leaps back; its wings carry it a few inches at a time until it performs a U-turn in the air and disappears upwards. You stand up and reach once more into your pocket. You find the apple – the bits of exposed flesh are now completely tan-coloured, and the skin looks macerated. You eat what's left of it, then set the hourglass core by the edge of the road. You think that perhaps you will never feel sadder than you do right now, and the enormity and romance of the thought bring you some comfort.

The lights are on in the kitchen. You can see your mother's narrow back at the table. Her head is resting on her hands and her yellow blob of a bun dangles at the nape of her neck. She never went to university – she got the grades but was too scared to leave home while the irregular war dragged on. Her brother went to the city two hours away, studied languages, went to discos on Friday nights and kissed girls and sometimes in secret kissed boys too. She stayed put, got a reception job in a health centre, became more anxious and angry. There is so much of your mother's past you've never put much effort into understanding.

On the table in front of her is the cordless handset of the phone, and next to that is her mobile. Next to that is your father's mobile. Last night, when he was downstairs whistling and folding towels and your mother was outside tugging weeds from between the kerbstones and you were supposed to be reading your history textbook, you went into his bedroom. You tapped in the code, 0206333 (your birthday, followed by three impatient 3s), and read the messages exchanged with an unsaved number.

17:48: DRINKS TOMORROW AT THE DEER'S LEAP? XX
17:50: Can't wait xxx

Your phone is still upstairs on your desk. You wonder what it will say when you turn it on. There will be missed calls from your mother and your father and the school, you suppose. Maybe there'll be a message from Rachael.

wtf happened to you today??

But maybe not.

Your father is pacing back and forth in front of the table. He's still dressed in the striped shirt and triangles of fabric have escaped from the waistband of his trousers. They hang along his belt like jubilee bunting. His black plastic wallet is on the counter. You peek your head around the edge of the window and you watch them. You wish that your actions existed for you alone.

You turn and drift towards the front door. Your arms and legs seem connected to your torso by coils, springing madly back and forth. The air is warm and the sky is a chromatic colour scale: red to orange to pink to pale beige. Your finger hovers over the rusted doorbell. You press it, and you are still waiting for the sound of the bell to crawl through the air and reach your ears when the door opens. Your father's eyes are puffy and red. You suspect they match yours. You look at one another, and you think for a moment about the history practice paper upstairs on your desk.

Quality of written communication will be assessed in all questions.

You wonder what happens now.

PART III

Eighteen years old – September 1st

You sit on the toilet airship, listening to the splashes. The sun streams blindingly bright through the translucent glass of the bathroom window – it lights up all the blue and green flickers of vein in your thighs. You stand up, wipe, and before dropping the handful of damp paper you peer into the bowl, looking for any traces of stringy white gum in the toilet's contents. You sigh, and flush.

Eighteen years old – September 2nd

'Hello?'
   'Hi, sunshine, what are you up to?'
   'I – who's this?'
   'It's your destiny calling – time to answer.'
   'What?'
   'It's Rachael, weirdo.'
   'Oh.'
The summer passed quietly – you received a fat fine and a two-year driving ban and were too ashamed to ever ask your mother for lifts. For your eighteenth birthday she

made a chocolate cake and your father took you to the cinema. He moved out two weeks ago – into Janine's home. You didn't sit your exams and in two days you will go back to school to repeat the year. A week ago you turned on your phone for the first time in three months and deleted all your contacts and messages and the twenty-four missed calls from Rachael. It felt good, like the entire history of yourself was bound up in names and typed words and you could erase all of it.

'I heard about all the shit that went down and I figured you might want some space. But then I also realized that I don't give a shit about what you want and I only give a shit about what I want, and here we are.'

'Oh.'

'I'm heading to Newcastle in a couple of weeks.'

'Oh.'

'Yeah. Mum's losing her head over it. Did you know you can buy collapsible saucepans?'

'No.'

'Well, you can, and I'm now the proud owner of four.'

'Wow.'

'I'll maybe even let you use one when you come visit.'

'Oh.'

'But enough about my new adventures as a kitchenware tycoon – what are you doing at the minute?'

'Nothing.'

She puts on an accent you think is supposed to be Texan. 'Well, knock me down with a collapsible saucepan!' Her voice returns to normal. 'C'mon, let's do something.'

Your mother walks in with an armful of laundry. She's

saying, 'Do you have anywhere to keep these—' when she notices you're on the phone. She freezes. She mouths, 'What is it?' and you shake your head and press the phone more tightly to your ear.

'Like what?'

'Whatever you fancy – the world's your oyster, princess.'

'We could go to the park?'

'Yes, perfect! I love it! Let's cut loose the grim tethers of polite society and go be forest nymphs.'

'OK,' and there's a brief silence. Rachael laughs.

'You know, I think it's your verbosity that I've missed the most.'

'Is Charlie coming?'

'What? God, no. Don't you know the benefit of leaving school is we can escape all that bullshit?'

'I'm not leaving school.'

'Semantics. Anyway, Charlie and I haven't spoken since the leaving party. I told her she's a massive bitch and she told me she's always thought I was boring.'

'Wow.'

'Right? As if anyone could think I was boring.'

You murmur your assent.

'So,' she begins to say, 'how was—'

You interrupt. 'There wasn't any gum in my shit.'

There is a pause. You think you can hear the slide projector of her memory clicking. 'Oh my God,' she says, 'I can't believe I forgot.'

'Seven years.'

'Wow.'

'Yeah.'

'But nothing?'

'Yeah. Nothing.'

'That's too bad.'

'Yeah.'

'But,' her tone is coaxing, 'maybe we don't need gum in your shit as a reason to celebrate life.'

'Maybe.'

There is another silence. You break it.

'So, the park?'

'Yes! I need to soak up some of that dry candour of yours.'

'OK.'

When you hang up your mother says, 'Rachael?' and you nod. You say, 'I didn't think we were still friends,' and your mother sets the laundry down on your bed and leans over to kiss your head. It occurs to you that you should wash your hair. She says, 'You know, maybe you're not alienating people as much as you think.'

Nineteen years old – September

'So that's you off tomorrow then?'

'Yeah.'

'Excited?'

'I suppose.'

You hear your father clearing his throat on the line. 'Do you want to come round for a cuppa before you go?'

You stare out of the window at a pigeon interrogating a crisp packet on the pavement. You have spent the last year avoiding going to your father's house – Janine's house. You hope your silence will answer for you.

'Or,' he tries again, 'I could come get you and we could go somewhere else?'

You exhale, relieved. 'OK.'

He exhales, relieved. 'OK. Fifteen minutes?'

'OK. I have the last bit of money.'

You've been working long shifts all year to gradually pay your parents back for the drink-driving fine. This morning you tried to give your mother a handful of notes. She shook her head and said, 'You can keep that,' and she squeezed your shoulder with one thin hand.

Your father's voice sounds absent-minded now, and you can picture him rummaging in his pockets for his car keys. 'What's that, love?'

'The fine. I have the money for you.'

'Never mind about that, love. Spend it on pints for your new university mates – we'll call it square.'

'OK.'

'See you soon.'

'OK.'

You wonder if your parents spoke – if they agreed that neither would accept the final payment, or if this was some tacit moment of unity. You lift your jacket off the coat stand in preparation. The pigeon abandons the crisp packet, goes elsewhere.

Nineteen years old – October 16th

The phone rings. You think, 'Someone is dead.'

The phone is a clumsy black landline that sits on your desk. The only person who ever uses it to contact you is your mother, who does so when you don't answer your mobile. She worries, more than ever, these days. You watch the handset vibrate in its cradle. You let it gurgle five times before answering.

The university you attend sits low on the various rankings – 4/10 for student satisfaction, and it is true that you seem to feel largely unsatisfied most days. The university is in a city an hour's flight and a half-hour bus journey away from home, and a twenty-minute bus journey away from any shops or nightclubs or museums, not that you often feel inclined to go to a shop or a nightclub or a museum. The campus is grey and insular, and when you sent photos to Rachael she messaged back 'Panopticon'. You live in a flat with three strangers all a year younger than you. On weeknights you gather with them in the kitchen to drink – they ask you if you've lost your virginity, what religion you are, if there is electricity where you come from. You are exotic here in a way that you initially liked, but are now exhausted by.

Someone *is* dead: your grandmother, of a pulmonary embolism. You rumble the idea around in your thoughts, try to decipher how you feel. You have never been entirely able to convince yourself that you love your grandmother. The thread that connects you to this taciturn and irritable and frighteningly old woman has always seemed too thin, fraying. She provokes the sort of conversation you have with people you are meeting for the first time – conversation that has the sole purpose of putting distance between you and the first 'hello'.

You will not travel home for the funeral. Your mother thinks this would be too disruptive and you are grateful to her for thinking this.

Nineteen years old – October 19th

On the day of the funeral you wake at 12 p.m. and while your flatmates are at lectures you venture into the kitchen and steal the bits of food they won't notice are missing – a bag of crisps from an eight-bag multipack, a slice of bread, a spoonful of peanut butter. You are careful to reshuffle the multipack so it doesn't look less full, to smooth out the new dents in the surface of the peanut butter.

That evening you sit in bed, eating biscuits from a packet you found in Jessica's cupboard. Jessica has shorn hair and short, dancer's legs. She ties polyester scarves around her throat and lends you clothes that don't fit you. She often comes into your room, uninvited, says, 'What do you think about this?' and pivots on her heels, her new, calf-length skirt swirling around her knees. You'll think about writing a number on a piece of paper, but you don't know these people yet, don't know how they'll respond to things. Instead you nod and say, 'Looks great,' and she says, 'I know, right?' She's at her boyfriend's place tonight and won't be back until tomorrow. Your mother texts to tell you that everything went smoothly – your father was in attendance, which pleased her. You take another biscuit. You wonder what food was served at the funeral.

Nineteen years old – February

'What is it, what's wrong?'

'I don't want to force it in.'

'No, do. Just push.'

His eyes are downcast and his brow is furrowed. He pushes. You close your eyes and picture him ripping apart the two strips of Velcro between your legs. You wince and he catches you. He looks annoyed.

'No, this isn't going to work.'

He pulls himself out and you feel the air whoosh in, find its way into the chasm. You feel it settle. Always the familiar pocket of cold air inside you, chilling your organs, your spine, your breath. You lie next to each other in silence. You wonder what you might say to make things better.

'I guess maybe you're just too big.'

You had wanted to sound playful, but you don't. It's a miscalculation.

'For fuck's sake – don't blame me! It's not my fault. You're the one who's too dry and too tight.'

'Oh.'

That evening you went for dinner at a mid-priced, pretend-French restaurant. On the menu the only words in French were the headings – *Entrées*, *Plats Principaux*, *Desserts*. The evening sky was navy and starlit and clear.

The air felt like sanitizer on your skin, so you asked plaintively to be allowed to sit outside. The waitress came out to take your order, her breath forming small fogs in front of her face.

'Hi' – a pause while he looked at her name badge – 'Karen. Is there any chance we could get one of these heaters turned on?' One finger was pointed upwards.

'Um' – the waitress was slim in the way you find to be consistent among waitresses, but that you don't resent – 'I don't think so. We normally don't use the heaters until the spring.'

'Well, what's the point in that? When it's warmer you'll need them less, whereas it's cold *now*.'

'Um, I'm sorry.'

You wanted to apologize to the waitress, but you hadn't. As he paid the bill he said to you, 'Although maybe you should pay in return for making me freeze my balls off all evening.'

His name is Robbie – he's doing a PhD in Human Rights. You met him in the Students' Union bar and he is not how you hoped he'd be. When you first saw him you were drawn to the purple scar of his repaired cleft lip. It seemed like a lightning-bolt-shaped marker of vulnerability, but you realize now that it was wrong of you to assume he would be something specific because of it.

You try, once more, to fix things.

'If we do this again I can try and sort it out before then.'

'What do you mean?'

'I don't know,' and you pause. You try to hear the words before you say them. 'I can get a dildo or something, and practise. I can try to make it less tight.'

He keeps his eyes pointed downwards, and you wonder if he is staring at his purposeless erection, still dressed in the condom. It pierces the air like a wonky flagpole. His tone is irritated.

'Jesus, no. Oh my God. Don't do that.'

Ten minutes later he is asleep. You turn over and put your hands between your legs and rub in a circular motion. You wait for the sting between your legs to dissipate, for the Velcro to shuffle back together. You decide you won't go to class tomorrow.

Twenty years old – March 23rd

'How's the new course going?'

'Yeah, better I think.'

She smiles at the road. 'Good.'

You are nearly one year into a different course from the one you began studying, but still at the same university. Where you study brings you neither shame nor pride, and if people ask, you are careful to tell them placidly, as though telling them you had cereal for breakfast. Your mother has cut her hair short, and you stare at where the small yellow bun used to be. Your suitcase rolls about on the back seat. She met you at the airport with a Dairy Milk Easter egg in her hands, her coat spattered with rain. The car passes a bus stop. The ad in the shelter is a picture of a man with a bloodied face.

'Mum?'

'Yes?'

'Would you drive me to get shot, if I had to get shot?'

'What's that?'

'If I had to go for a punishment shooting, would you drive me?'

'I can't believe you're still asking me these sorts of questions.'

'But . . . ?'

'But what?'

'If I did, would you drive me?'

She sighs. 'I suppose so.'

'I mean, if you didn't want to I could take a bus, but it might be nicer if you took me.'

She fights her smile. 'I promise that if you are having a punishment shooting, I will drive you.'

'Thanks, Mum.'

'You're welcome.'

'Do they shoot you in the back of the knees or the front?'

'I think it's more just somewhere in the vicinity of the knees.'

'It would probably be easier to get purchase at the back of the knees.'

'Like I said, I think it's more that they just shoot you in the legs.'

'I still think I'd rather get shot in the hand.'

'They wouldn't give you that option.'

'That's not very nice of them.'

She laughs. 'Strange, that.'

Twenty years old – March 27th

Rachael has come home for Easter with an eyebrow pier-cing: a small gold hoop that lights up the smooth skin on her brow. You put your hand on her chin and turn her head from side to side.

'That's enough with the manhandling.'

'Was it sore?'

'As sore as it ever is, getting a brand-new hole in your face.'

'Do you like it?'

'Of course I do. Mum hates it though – she says I look like a loyalist paramilitary. I was like, "Gotta fit in with the English crowd, don't I?"'

'I was thinking more nineties pop star.'

'Not entirely against either, to be honest.'

'Do you like it there?'

'It's great.'

'Why's it great?'

'I don't know, the people, the books, the gentle internal thrum of feeling like your life has a purpose.'

'I suppose.'

'Why, do you not like it? I thought this new course was going to alleviate every fear and uncertainty you've ever known in your fraught little life.'

You keep your eyes on the small gold hoop. 'I guess I just had an image in my head.'

She crosses one leg over the other, affects a therapist pose. 'What image was that, then?'

'Walking across a campus in autumn, leaves blowing about my legs, holding books to my chest, wearing a big scarf.'

'And it's not like that?'

'Well, autumn ends, doesn't it?'

She laughs. 'I suppose it does.'

'And you have to open the books and read them, at some point.'

'That too.'

She passes you a plate loaded with cubes of cheese. You've always liked Rachael's house; the abundance of plates covered with small portions of food. You take a dark-yellow piece.

'Rachael?'

'Yes, buttercup?'

'If you had to get shot anywhere, where would you get shot?'

She stops chewing and tilts her head. The light lands on the hoop. 'Foot,' she says, after a while.

'Why?'

'I think I would tell people I did it to myself to avoid military service. I've always wanted to be seen as a glamorous coward.'

'Wow.'

'Stop staring at my eyebrow, it's unsettling.'

'I don't think I'll ever be able to look anywhere else.'

She flings the back of her hand to her forehead. 'Oh, cruel fate!' Her suitcase sits in the corner, half packed, half unpacked.

Twenty-one years old – March

You can see the reflection of yourself in the glass pane on his front door. It's warm, too warm for March, and you got dressed in a rush and you are regretting the jumper and coat and trainers. Your hair is furry and dry at the ends and greasy at the roots. You have a large patch of dry skin on your cheek. You arrange your hair to try and hide it, try to ignore how disgusted you are by your body. You ring the doorbell.

You woke at 11:20 a.m. to an email inviting you to his house at twelve. He is a visiting lecturer, Australian, and although he told the class to call him Laurence, you cannot bring yourself to, and so avoid addressing him by name entirely. He has a high-pitched voice and a patchy moustache, long legs but a round abdomen. He has published one book of critical theory and one day you found a typo in it: 'form' instead of 'from'. Until this morning he had expressed no particular interest in you, which is something you thought you appreciated. He is leaving tomorrow.

He opens the door and your hands immediately return to your hair. He says, 'Hi,' and asks how you are, and it doesn't seem to matter when you don't tell him how you are. He takes your hand and leads you down the hall. He commences undressing you, and soon you are standing in the middle of his bedroom, naked, with your arms wrapped around your soft and sagging middle and your eyes squinting at the light coming through the blinds. He calls you beautiful and sexy, and you know that this is a case of youth equating to beauty; of availability equating to beauty; of willingness equating to beauty. You let him press you

against a wall and put his hands on your breasts. You wonder at your own passivity. He holds your head in his hands
and looks at you and you try to angle your head to the side
because you know you don't look good face-on. He turns
your head back to face him, firmly.

You put your hand to his trousers and notice that he isn't
hard. He smiles and says, 'I'm a little embarrassed.' You
say, 'Why?' and it is the first time you've spoken. He says,
'Because I don't have a throbbing erection to fuck you
with,' and the apology, the pornographic description of his
own penis, the erroneous 'fuck' on a Wednesday afternoon,
all make you wish you were somewhere else.

He pushes his fingers inside you and you apologize for
how your hair looks, because it seems like you should apologize to match his apology. He puts his hands back to your
hair and kisses you, but it's too soft and wet, like sushi, and
you wonder if it's something he saw in a film once and
decided to copy. On the chest of drawers is a photograph of
his wife and daughter, and you wish you were in Australia
with them. You wish you were them.

You get dressed with your back turned to him. He is lying
on top of the bed. The duvet has no cover on it, and the
sight of it makes you almost unbearably sad. His trousers are
bunched around his ankles and his shirt is pushed up around
his nipples. The last thing he says to you is, 'Thank you,
sweet girl.' By the front door is another chest of drawers
with all the drawers removed; on top is an unplugged lamp
with the cord tied up, a passport, and a wallet. You open the
wallet. You take out twenty-five pounds in notes, leaving
him a ten-pound note and two pound coins. You walk out.

Twenty-two years old – March

'Is that – what the fuck is going on with your face? Is that ringworm?'

Rachael has been living in London for nine weeks. She has a Master's degree now and is working as a waitress in a Norwegian cafe. You knock on the door and a curl of paint that looks like beef carpaccio rolls towards the floor. The hallway smells like urine and burnt meat. You cover half your face with hair so only one eye can see when she opens the door.

'No. I think it's something else.'

As she looks at you her lips stretch and try to touch the doorframe on either side. She turns and you follow her in.

'It really looks like ringworm. Gran used to get it from working with the cows.' She pauses and laughs. 'You'd better not be bringing ringworm into my flat.'

You look around.

'Seems like it's already here.'

'Fuck off.'

There is a crispy-looking sock hanging from the smoke alarm. On a coffee table with a missing leg (a water-wrinkled dictionary has been put in its place) there is a pizza box. A thimble-sized bluebottle wanders across it.

'How did you end up with ringworm?'

'It's not ringworm.'

'Then what is it?'

'Impetigo, I think.'

'Seriously? Gran had that too! In the nursing home! I thought only old people and tiny kids got that – we weren't allowed to bring my baby cousin to see her.'

The sink makes a hollow aluminium rattle when you set a glass in it. The water comes out cloudy. Rachael's grey shorts have a rip in them. She looks frail.

'You have, like, the worst immune system.'

You think of the web page you looked at this morning.

You are more likely to develop a fungal infection if you:
- are very young or very old
- have type 1 diabetes
- have a medical condition that weakens your immune system, such as

Not today.

Every few months you wake at 4 a.m. with bad thoughts. You Google symptoms and prognoses until the sky lightens and your eyes ache from staring at the blue screen. You wish you had someone to convince you that this is irrational, but that would require telling someone, and telling someone would mean committing to the truth of what has happened to you. You would be given a title that you're not sure you want, that you're not sure you've earned. You shake your head to empty it.

'It's fine. I'll wash the sheets and stuff and I'll get antibiotics when I go home.'

'OK, scabby.'

'Shut up.'

She nudges you out of the way with her hips. She fills a mug which says *Best Dad! Top Dad! No. 1 Dad!* with misty water. She sniffs it, then drinks. She screws up her face.

'So,' she hoists herself up on to the counter and pokes

your arm with a clammy toe. 'Guess who I bumped into when I was at home last weekend?'

'Mr Hughes?'

'What? No. I didn't mean for you to actually guess, you little weirdo.'

'Who then?'

'Charlie!'

'Oh.'

'Yeah! I was in the supermarket getting Mum some of those creepy little gherkins she likes and Charlie was floating about the magazines.'

'Wow.'

'She's moved home. I think she works in one of those nice salons by the river. You know the ones? Anyway, she's totally different now.'

'Oh yeah?'

'Yeah! Whatever meds she's on, she's almost nice now, like she isn't capable of being a bitch any more.'

'Wow.'

Rachael laughs and swings her legs. 'Maybe try to hide your pleasure a tiny bit.'

You open and close the kitchen cupboards. There's a tin of Tesco baked beans and a box of Coco Pops and a bottle of bleach. You walk over to the defeated sofa and lift up a cushion – underneath is a dirty plate crusted with swirls of dried ketchup. You hold it up.

'Look, ringworm.'

'Fuck off.'

'I'm not pleased.'

'Of course you are.'

'Why would I be?'

'She was always pretty mean to you.'

You keep your voice flat. 'Was she?'

'Don't play dumb.' She shakes her head vehemently and her hips wiggle along the granite countertop. 'God, it must be exhausting for you.'

You keep your eyes on the fossilized patterns of red. 'What?'

'Never forgetting anything.'

There is silence for a moment. You set the plate upside down on top of the pizza box. 'So what happened?'

'I don't really know. I mean, I'd heard from Beth a while ago that she was smoking a scary amount of weed in Manchester, which apparently is just de rigueur up there, but then she started on MDMA as well, and maybe mushrooms, and God knows what else. I think she was dating a girl who did some dealing on the side. Anyway, I messaged Beth after I saw her and Beth said her housemate found her screaming in the kitchen, throwing cups at the wall and writing on the curtains with a Sharpie.'

'Wow.'

'I know. So her meds keep her chill but they also make her . . . It's a bit like talking to someone who's wearing a space helmet, like everything you say to her is muffled and there's a time delay in her response.'

'Did she get the security deposit back on the house?'

'Jesus. Not the point.'

'I guess.'

Rachael pronounces 'de rigueur' ironically: *doo rigger.* She pours the rest of the milky water into the sink and pulls at a loose nail on her toe. You drift towards her.

'How's journalism going?'

Rachael grunts. 'Uh. Shit. There's no paid work, and even unpaid work is super hard to get. I spent ages writing this bullshit listicle called "The 10 Sexiest Bars in East London" and the editor was a dick because I used the wrong form of "your" or something, *once*, and then he didn't even publish it.'

'What makes a bar sexy?'

Rachael sighs and continues to twist the loose toenail. 'I don't know.'

'Is it the drinks or the lighting or do the people in it have to be doing sexy things?'

'I don't know.'

'Did you feel sexy when you were in the bars?'

'Please stop.'

'Or do the people in the bar have to be sexy before they get there?'

'You can stop now.'

You start swivelling your hips. 'Is this sexy? Can I go to the sexy bars now?'

She laughs and shakes her head. 'Seriously, stop. Not the point.' The toenail comes loose. She holds it close to her eye.

You stop gyrating. 'I guess.'

'So, anyway, I heard there's some good PR jobs going at this firm that's opening offices all over the place, so I reckon I might go somewhere else soon.'

'Wow.'

'Plus, you know the guy I mentioned, Greg? Well, we were messaging the other day and he said he wished I lived closer so he could see more of me, so that might be worth exploring.'

You lift the plate off the pizza box and the bluebottle veers wildly from side to side. Inside the box are two congealed slices; they look like they're made of wet clay. You lift one and Rachael squeals.

'Don't! That's, like, three days old! And it's not even mine, one of the others brought it in.'

'I'm hungry.'

'No wonder you have ringworm.'

'It's not ringworm.'

'OK, scabby. So, what do you want to do tomorrow?'

'Nothing that involves people seeing my face.'

Rachael leaps off the counter and skips to the bin. She lifts a paper plate off the top, folds it in two and tears it. She holds the half-plate over her face so you can only see one eye, half a nose, half a mouth.

'We could always make you a *Phantom of the Opera* mask.'

'I'm tired.'

'OK, OK, one drink, then bed.' Rachael pulls a half-empty bottle of gin from behind a box propped against the wall. The box has a picture of a woman with mid-length blonde hair smiling lovingly at an ironing board. Rachael picks a cobweb off the bottle. She points it at you. 'But if I wake up all ringwormy I'm going to kill you.'

Twenty-three years old – June

His hand edges along the picnic table and his thumb moves along your wrist. Your breath stalls in your throat at the sudden contact. You have just turned twenty-three, and an hour ago you met him in the Students' Union bar. His name is Shaun, and when he said, 'Feels weird to be finished, right?' you smiled and agreed.

Once, when Rachael had come to visit, you asked her, 'How do you get someone to want to have sex with you?' And she laughed and said, 'All you have to do is touch literally any part of their body with your thumb.' You had been sceptical, but now you think perhaps it's the most meaningful gesture in the world.

He keeps his eyes forward, and you ignore all the parts of you that are itching: the eyelash bothering the corner of your eye; the bits of hair that are pulled too tight into your fraying rhizome of a hairstyle. You don't want to do anything to stop him from stroking your hand like this.

When he asks if you want to go somewhere with him you want to say 'No', because you'd much rather the two of you stayed on this bench, in this moment that feels loaded but that hasn't been spoiled yet. There is an enormous skip twenty yards away and students walk up in groups to throw away their hefty stacks of revision notes and their empty beer cans. Your first final was two days ago – you left after twenty minutes. Your second was this morning. Your alarm went off at 8:50. You switched it off, turned over, went back to sleep.

The sky is somewhere between lilac and royal blue, and the impenetrable wall of trees beyond the green is outlined with the red of the now-disappeared sun. You wish you could stay in this moment, with your most recent failures a secret and this man's soft thumb making you feel wanted. He turns to you.

'Did you hear me? Let's go somewhere.'

★

Campus is in darkness. Assorted construction equipment and postgraduate Fine Art sculptures are scattered about the place. They look like monsters. You tell him you need to use the toilet. He squeezes your ass and says, 'Don't be long,' and you stumble away, nearly tripping over the pebbled border at the edge of the grass. You don't recognize the buildings at night, and every door is locked. You stumble around, pushing handles at random and peering about for any electric light. It's getting darker. Eventually, you give up and wedge yourself into a corner between the Arts and Media faculty and the library. You bunch your skirt in your hands and start pissing. It splashes on to the tops of your feet and up your shins. You press your back to the wall and walk your feet out, till your torso and legs form a 135-degree angle. You've lost momentum now though, and the piss just trickles down your thighs before dripping off your knees. You try to shake it off your legs but when you drop your skirt the fabric sticks to the wettest patches. You jump up and down on the spot for a while, attempting to dry it. You wander back.

Your mouth tastes like cheap beer and your thoughts feel slow. You stop and rest for a moment against an enormous chess piece with bird's wings. You look around, seeing only wide patches of nothing. You take the hem of your skirt and flap it up and down. You massage the dampness over your crotch, and when your hands come away sticky you dry them on your top. When he finds you his voice is impatient and he pulls you away, to an old stone tenement near a car park. It's full of chairs and dissembled bandstands and detritus. He pushes you against the wall and his hand goes up your skirt, hurriedly. You miss the gentleness of before.

He puts his mouth to your ear and whispers, 'Oh my God, you're so fucking wet for me,' and you're relieved to realize that he doesn't know it's just piss, and maybe some sweat.

Twenty-four years old – August

There is a couple across the aisle from you on the train. You try to ignore them. You shuffle the papers in your lap, reread the practice interview questions – what *does* exceptional customer service mean to you? The words sit in your head until they mutate into shapelessness, and you turn your eyes back to the couple. You watch as the man next to the window twists in his seat and lifts his legs – in indigo shorts – and drapes them across the other man's lap. The other man, who you now take to be the more grounded and sturdy of the two – the scaffolding, the ballast, the spine – places his hand wide over the bare shin and rubs up and down. The breezy, slighter man whispers something in his ear, and you watch them so intently you think you can feel his lips fuzzing at your earlobe. When you get up you ask if they would mind watching your bag. They smile. They nod.

You go into the phone-box-sized cubicle of the train toilet and lock the door. You pull your trousers and knickers down around your ankles and put your index finger to your labia and find damp. You curl your finger up inside you, stroke the curved ridge that feels like the skin of a strawberry. You go deeper, and the hot walls within you make space. You grip the sink with your other hand and bend over slightly. You ease your index finger out and slide it against your middle finger. When both are wet you move them back and forth over the soft, fleshy barcode of your clitoris. You spread your legs as wide as they can go and you speed up. You keep going. After a while your body tenses. A constricted hotness starts to build deep inside you – patches of pink appear on your thighs. You keep going, until something ignites beneath your hand and your eyes close and your right knee shakes. You keep going until you can't. A high-pitched moan pushes its way out of you and you leak on to your fingers. For a moment you don't move, and then you lean back against the wall, panting. You tune back in to the sound of the train buzzing over the tracks.

Twenty-four years old – December

'When can we leave?'

'After this drink, I promise. I just said I'd put in an appearance and throw some money in the ol' missionary bucket.'

You look over at Bethany, who's angelic and conspicuous in a white turtleneck. 'Do you think she has her rosary beads on under there?'

'Who cares?'

'Did she ever get Charlie a set?'

'Stop being Rain Man.'

'OK.'

'Oh God. Right, OK, some guys are coming over. Be nice.'

'OK.'

'But not silent.'

'OK.'

'Nice and not silent.'

'OK.'

The men are dressed in beige trousers and cable-knit jumpers. They look like off-duty pharmacists. They stop at the edge of the table. One of them smiles.

'So, what are you girls looking so serious about?'

Rachael gestures at you with her head and he turns to you. You look at him.

'We're discussing whether the film *Pompeii* warranted a sequel. My feeling is: yes.'

Rachael lets out a loud laugh. The man peers at you.

'What?'

'Never mind.'

Rachael kneads your ankle with her boot and mouths 'Be nice'. They look at you both expectantly. You take a mouthful of white wine and then a mouthful of Pepsi. The two sit separately in your mouth, like water and oil.

The Deer's Leap hasn't changed. There's a spray-paint coating of frost on the ground in the smoking area and the seven picnic tables are dressed in green tarpaulin – they look like sleeping animals. You and Rachael sit opposite one another in a booth. Scattered around the bar are yellow collection buckets with Sellotaped-on photos of Bethany and her fiancé – a short man with veneers. Rachael has been invited to their wedding; you have not. By the door is a sandwich board with a blown-up version of the same picture, with 'Private Charity Function' on a sheet of paper Blu-Tacked to it. Rachael has a glass of lemonade in front of her – you are the only one drinking. The slightly more handsome man places his hands on the table.

'So, how do you two know Beth and John?'

You close your eyes and listen to Rachael talk.

'Oh, we went to school with Bethany. Long time ago. We're both home for Christmas so we figured we'd stop by and support her.'

'That's kind of you. It's nice you all kept in touch.'

You open your eyes.

'I haven't spoken to her since I was nineteen.'

'Oh?'

'She invited me to a prayer meeting.'

'Oh, that's cool.'

'I think she thought I needed spiritual intervention.'

'Oh?'

'I didn't go.'

'Oh.'

Rachael lets out another laugh. The man looks down at the table, his mouth slightly open. He takes a sharp intake of breath and then slides into the booth beside Rachael. She sidles towards the wall, grimacing at you. You close your eyes again and feel a change in pressure in the cushion as the other man sits next to you. The handsome one rubs his hands together.

'So, are either of you members of the church?'

'No.' Rachael coughs pointedly and you open your eyes. 'We don't live here any more.'

'No, I mean any church.'

'Still no.'

'That's too bad. We're doing a series of protests a few weeks from now, down south, with a whole bunch of congregations. You could still come though – you don't have to be churchgoers to protest evil.'

You tilt your head to the side. 'What evil are you protesting?'

'The new abortion law.'

You feel Rachael's legs stiffen against yours. You speak slowly.

'Oh. Right.'

He smiles excitedly. 'Please feel free to join. We need all hands on deck.'

Rachael's hands have disappeared under the table.

'Well' – you pause – 'I imagine that will be a lovely day out for everyone.'

His smile shrinks. Now it's his head that tilts slightly. 'It's not a day out, exactly. This is important work we're doing.'

Rachael stays silent, her eyes downcast. You take a larger sip of wine. You try to make your face go thoughtful.

'I guess you could say that about anything though, really. Cirque du Soleil. Or pet therapy.'

His mouth twists. 'This isn't a joke, you know.'

'I agree – pet therapy is a crucial field.'

'I'm not saying I'm judging them.'

'What's to judge? Cats need CBT too.'

'I mean the women.'

'What women?'

'Having abortions.'

'You're not judging them?'

'No. I just think the law needs to change.'

'The law just got changed.'

'It needs to change back.'

'Why's that, then?'

'Because it's—' He stops, takes a breath, paces himself. 'It's evil and thoughtless. The act of abortion is evil and thoughtless.'

'That's what I've always heard about abortion. That it's thoughtless. Hey, shall we get a pizza? No, I think I'd sooner have a nice big abortion.'

Rachael's mouth itches towards a half-smile. You wonder at this version of yourself. It occurs to you that this is probably how you behave on dates – loud and performative and secondary-school-theatre confrontational. The man's frown has not moved.

'You're not – you're not *pro*-abortion?'

You wink at him. You realize as you do that you're not sure you've ever winked before. He leans forward.

'You can't possibly condone the killing of babies.'

Under the table, Rachael's fingers find yours. You lean forward too. You whisper.

'I love killing babies.'

'Don't say that.'

'I do. Give me a club, a mallet, a nice big pickaxe. That's just a Saturday afternoon for me.'

Rachael starts to vibrate on the seat. The man's mouth is downturned, incredulous.

'You're horrible.'

You wink again. He shakes his head and gets up and walks away, hunched. The man sitting next to you stays on the bench, silent. He starts to pick at his fingernails. Rachael looks at him for a moment, then back to you. She raises her eyebrows and squeezes your knee.

'I'm going to pee and then we can go, OK?'

She gives the man another confused look as she slides

out of the booth. You look at your empty wine glass. He clears his throat and turns his wide shoulders towards you. He smiles.

'I think I'm going to head home soon.'

'OK.'

'Would you like to come with me?'

'Home with you?'

'Yeah. For some fun.'

He has a scar at the edge of his hairline: an inch of puckered pink. It looks like half a worm. You look at it for a few moments before speaking.

'For sex, you mean?'

He laughs. 'If you want to be blunt about it.'

You turn back towards the empty seat opposite you. You pick up your wine glass and hold it to your mouth, even though it's empty.

'So' – you pause – 'it's kind of a Sunday carvery approach to religion then, huh?'

'What?'

'Nothing.'

Rachael makes her way back across the room. You lift your bag off the floor.

The man next to you clears his throat. 'So, what do you think?'

Rachael stands a foot from the table. She nods towards the door. You start to wriggle out of the booth, using your hips to forcibly nudge him along the cushion. When all three of you are standing you turn to him.

'I can't have sex tonight, I'm afraid. I have to go kill some babies.'

The music has been turned down and the wine has turned

your voice up. People, standing in clusters, look over. Bethany, standing by the bar, screws up her face. Rachael laughs and gives her a wave before pulling you towards the door. Outside, she puts her head on your shoulder. There is the sound of a gritter in the distance. You wrap your arms around her.

Twenty-four years old – January

'What do you think?'

'That's not what – I asked you first.'

He frowns. 'I know, but what do *you* think?'

You have just slept with the skinny man in bed next to you. His name is Ryan and the sex is always the same – him on top, huffing noisily like a badger. It doesn't hurt to have sex with him, and the first time you were relieved at the ease with which you were able to take him inside you. You hoped that pleasure might follow.

He has large, brown eyes and he wears contact lenses on special occasions – he wore them to the office Christmas party and to his grandmother's birthday. He never wears them on your dates. He squints at you – his tortoiseshell glasses are somewhere on the dusty wood floor.

'I like you.'

You hear yourself say this, and immediately wonder if it's true. You sometimes think your feelings are conjured into existence only by speaking out loud – your body's way of trying to stop you from being dishonest.

'I like you too.' He pauses. 'But I wonder if it's maybe more as a friend?'

'Right. So you want to stop seeing each other?'

'Well,' and he seems deep in thought, and you wonder if he's actually just trying to make out the blurry impressionist postcards Blu-Tacked to your wardrobe door. 'What do you think?'

You are working as a receptionist at a large, faceless consulting firm; a temporary contract while a woman is on maternity leave. He works in their finance department, and you met at the Christmas party. You stood by the bar and smiled at people you sort of recognized; he wore tight-fitting trousers he later told you were from the Primark women's department. You have been dating for six weeks. Two weeks in, you told your mother over the phone that you were seeing someone and she seemed pleased. After the phone call you texted your father and told him what films you'd watched recently – *The Lobster*, *The Purge*, *The Day After Tomorrow* – and whether they were good. Your parents have been living separately now for six years.

You stare at Ryan's profile. You imagine pressing his head into the poorly painted white wall. Pressing and pressing and pressing until something in his skull gives and his head spreads flat and wide across the white, filling in the cracks and covering the smudges. You're not even sure he would object.

You try again. 'No, I'm asking what you want to do.'

'I like you.'

'OK.'

'So, what do you think?'

'You like me?'

'Um. Yes.'

'But as a friend?'

'Yeah.'

'So, I guess we should stop seeing each other then?'

'Is that what you want to do?'

'It seems like that's what you want to do.'

'OK, if you think that's best.'

He offers to sleep on the sofa, and you say no, he might as well stay. The apartment is small and the sofa in the combined kitchen–living room is chaotic with broken springs. You are struggling to pay your rent every month and for a moment you imagine him moving in with you – the two of you sharing the rent and a bed and a life. You shake the thought away and roll over to face the wall.

You wake up in the middle of the night. You are both lying flat on your backs next to one another and you think of images from your history textbook: the laid-out bodies of murdered villagers. You run your fingers along the peaks and troughs of his rib cage and when he grunts you slide your hand under his boxer shorts and take his cock in your hand. He responds to this with neither reluctance nor enthusiasm. He finds a condom under a pillow – you always insist on a condom. He rips it open with his teeth, rolls on top of you. You listen to the familiar *huff huff huff* as he thumps at you. His eyes are pointed straight ahead, and you wonder what the wall looks like through his foggy eyes. You wonder if he is imagining his own brains and blood and eyes and skin plugging the canyons in the cheap paint.

Twenty-four years old – March

Three days after Rachael's surgery you go to visit her.

The room is square and bright and lemon-coloured. Rachael is sitting up in bed. The skin under her eyes is blue-tinged, and you can see deep grooves in the skin on her lips. You peer at her chest.

'Is it sore?'

'Yeah, course, but the painkillers are good.'

'When do the bandages come off?'

'Tomorrow. I'm pretty scared about it – they said it'll be weeks before the bruising and swelling go all the way down.'

'They look pretty big.'

'Right? Although some of that's probably the puffiness.'

'Are you worried the swelling will just keep going down and down and down until you realize they aren't actually any bigger at all?'

'No, I'm not worried about that.'

The room has three yellow walls and one white wall with large French windows with painted white frames. You can smell bleach. On a table by the bed are Rachael's phone and seven greetings cards. You pick one up: *Get Well Soon!* in cursive, and some splodgy purple and orange and white tulips in a splodgy vase. Inside: 'Hope to see you back at work soon. We miss you. Theresa xxxxxx'. You put the card back on the edge of the table; it leans precariously.

'Does Theresa know why you're in here?'

Rachael lets out a laugh that is short and hoarse and metallic, like a microwave door being closed.

'God, that bitch would have a field day if she knew. I told her I was getting my tonsils out.'

'What if she asks to look in your throat?'

'Why would she do that? People don't do that.'

'I suppose.'

'She'll probably wonder why I've taken so much time off, but I can just say I caught a bug or something. Hospitals are full of bugs, right? I swear my gran always came out sicker than she went in.'

You nod and wander around the room, lifting items and putting them back: a single daffodil in a vase; a laminated sheet with fire safety instructions; a copy of *Heat*. You open the door of the toilet and peer in.

'Don't go in there, I was a bit sick before you came.'

The bleach in the air mingles with something else. You close the door. In the corner, by the windows, is a cornflower-blue armchair with two smiling teddy bears sitting on it: a white one and a brown one. They're sewn together at the paws, surgically hugging. You hold them up and wiggle them at Rachael.

'Were these bears patients here?'

That microwave-door laugh again – *thunk*. You set the bears down.

'Has Greg been to see you?'

'Course he has. He was here this morning. He had about a million questions for the nurse' – and here she puts on a gruff, deep voice that sounds nothing like Greg's – ' "*When* will she be healed, are you *sure* the surgery went OK, *what* do we do if anything *bad* happens?" ' She stares at the outlines of flowers on her duvet cover. 'He was fucking relentless.'

'Did he ask how you were?'

'Course he did! God, this was *my* idea, you know. Don't get all . . . you-y. You know, all overthinky.' She frowns. 'Want me to ask the nurse to get you a nice sedative?'

'That's OK – I only eat organic sedatives.'

'Fancy bitch.'

'Fancy sedate bitch.'

'Fancy irate bitch.'

'Fancy prostrate bitch.'

'Fancy ingrate bitch.'

You sit on the blue chair; it exhales. You stare at the scruffy lampshade with gold embroidery. Rachael looks at you, her hands resting just below her bandaged cleavage.

'The decor is pretty nice when you go private, huh?'

'Yeah, I suppose' – you pause – 'if you're into yellow.'

'Shut up, bitch.' Her heart doesn't seem in it.

You watch as she reaches over, slowly, to lift her phone. As she lies back on the pillows she winces and you wonder if this is your cue to leave. To get to the clinic you took a forty-five-minute train and then the wrong bus and then a corrective bus and then the right bus and then walked for twenty minutes. You wish Greg were here so he might feel obliged to book you an Uber home. Greg is thirty-one and a solicitor and wealthy and handsome. He always looks at you like he wants to ruffle your hair.

The first few bars of 'Crazy' by Patsy Cline start, and Rachael sets her phone down again, her eyes half closed. She smiles.

'There was a mad woman in the room next door who was in for, like, her third facelift, and she was obsessed with this song. She'd play it about five times a day. I heard her say to a nurse once, "Patsy was a *real* doll." Anyway, now I can't stop listening to it.'

You pick at the thread between the bears' paws.

'Do you and Greg ever talk about the other thing?'

Rachael's eyes open.

'Can we not?'

'Sorry.'

'It's done with. We weren't ready. *I* wasn't ready. And anyway' – she becomes suddenly wild – 'lucky it happened over here, eh? Eh?!'

You pull at another loose bear thread. You say nothing. She slaps the duvet with both hands.

'Come on! You're meant to be making me feel better, for fuck's sake.' She smirks. 'So, how's your job?' And when you say nothing she stops smiling and pats the edge of her bed. You sit down and she presses her face into your hair. Patsy Cline drifts through the room like a bluebottle.

As you get up to leave Rachael says, 'You know, you're a real doll for coming,' and you say, 'No, you're the real doll,' and she says, 'No, no, *you're* the real doll.' Her skin is pallid and damp and you wish Greg were there to rub her back as she leans over the toilet bowl. As you walk through the double wooden doors of the clinic you wonder if the surgeon got rid of the old lining of her breasts before cramming in the new, artificial filling, or if the two are allowed to intermingle; clean, clear jelly on top of messy, yellow fat.

Eight weeks ago she took a pill in the clinic, then another pill twenty-four hours later. She had some cramping, some bleeding, that was it. You walk across the small car park and past the fat, breast-shaped shrubs next to the fat stone columns at the entrance. You turn in the direction of the bus stop. Patsy Cline's voice croons in your head.

Twenty-five years old – September 17th

'Tell me something you've never told anyone.'

Sam is twenty-five. His words are slurred and his shirt is too tight and metallic purple. The nightclub is wallpapered with a clashing shade of purple and it has patches of raised velour in a third shade of purple. Your back is pressed against the wall and you stroke one of the raised patches with your palm. He dips his head and kisses your neck and the bristles of his shaved chin abrade your skin. When he comes back up for air you scratch at the irritation. His eyes are unfocused and you can see his chest through the oval-shaped portholes between shirt buttons. He falls forward and his mouth slams against yours. The music is loud and thumping and wordless. He shouts it again.

'Tell me something you've never told anyone.'

In work that day the other receptionists presented you with an enormous red velvet cupcake as a leaving present. The maternity contract is up and you are flying home in two days – you haven't saved any money and you can't afford to renew the lease on the poorly painted flat with the impressionist postcards on the wall. You spent your last day ignoring the flashing lights on the phone and flicking through a nature magazine, licking dried buttercream from the corners of your mouth.

Tonight everyone is out for an audit manager's birthday. You've tagged along. Another receptionist said, 'To us it's really your leaving party – we hate the accounts wankers,' and you wanted to cry with gratitude. You met Sam while standing at the bar. You put your mouth closer to where you think his ear is – he's wearing a sagging, woolly hat, even though the atmosphere in the club is congested with body heat.

'Like what?'

He sways in front of you. 'Anything. Something nobody knows.'

You stroke the velvety wallpaper.

'When I was seventeen a man shoved his cock in my ass.'

You look at him – his eyes are downcast. The silence between you seems furious and for ever.

At last his eyes find yours and he blinks twice, slowly. His eyelids droop. He falls against you again and his tongue trails along your bottom lip. He puts his hand to your crotch and rubs, gently. When he pulls away he keeps his fingers pressed between your legs. The music seems even louder, now. You wonder if he's choosing his words carefully. He hiccups, then burps, then hiccups again. His breath smells acidic.

'Tell me something you've never told anyone.'

Your earlier confession forgotten, or unheard entirely, Sam seems less bleary-headed now. The music is loud enough that you don't have to say much and you are happy to watch his lips move and nod at intuitive moments. Three of the receptionists give you thumbs up behind his back before trooping to the toilet, one organism. When he goes to the bar you watch a girl rearrange her friend's cleavage under her tight dress. Both sway on their high heels. Sam returns, and you drink deeply from the pint glass. He shouts over the bass-heavy music.

'I'm staying at my friend's place tonight – it's a bit of a distance away and it's going to be pretty crowded.'

'Right.'

He reaches up and pulls his hat off for the first time. His hair flops around his ears and you stare at it. It's shoulder-length, fair and gently curling. You move your eyes to his lips, notice for the first time how thin they are. He scratches his head.

'So, we can't really go back there, but I spotted an alley round the corner. It looked pretty private.'

You move your eyes back to his hair. He wraps one tendril around his finger.

'Right.'

'So, you want to go check it out?'

'The alley?'

He smiles. 'Yeah.'

Your cheeks become hot, everywhere else on your body clammy. You watch his finger make a maypole out of his hair. You nod, and he vanishes his beer in seconds. He takes his hand away from his head and puts it to his chest. He belches.

'I have to use the toilet, and then we can go, yeah?'

You nod again and he smiles. He gets up from the table. When you see the bathroom door close behind him you stand up and walk past the girls in the tight dresses and out the door. The bouncer says, 'Thanks, love,' and then you run. The night air is clean on your skin, and you don't stop running.

Twenty-five years old – September 19th

'And of course if you don't buy enough sweets and chocolate and things it always gets to about 9 p.m. and you think, "Oh, maybe I'm out of the woods," but then the bigger kids start showing up, the ones who are far too old to dress up but still do, the ones who might tip over your bin or take a shit on your porch or scare your cat if you don't have anything to give them, and I guess maybe you should have offered fewer sweets to the kids who came earlier because then you might have some left over for the bigger assholes, but the little kids are who Halloween is really for, right? And you don't want to say to a Darth Vader the height of your knee, "Oh, you can only have one chocolate bar, please return that fun-size Twirl so I don't have to worry about a fifteen-year-old in a sombrero shitting on my front step at 9 p.m., and also you're, like, four, do you even know what a Darth Vader is?" So of course you wind up buying far, far too much.'

The static voice over the intercom tells the crew to prepare for landing. A bell dings and the lights in the cabin dim. You stare resolutely at your upright tray table as the woman next to you keeps talking.

'So you buy about six bags of miniatures, and then of course that's the year that it's raining or there's a stomach bug outbreak or some idiot hosts a drive-in cinema in a field and so nobody shows up except for maybe four or five groups of kids, and you try to offload the extra stuff on them but of course kids these days can afford to be fucking discerning about the chocolate they take for free from strangers, and you know what none of the kids want? Chomps. You ever had a Chomp? Fucking Chomps. It's like a Curly

Wurly but more solid. So I get left at the end of the night with a huge bowl full of nothing but fucking Chomps, and they're horrible, they're completely horrible, and I suppose I could just throw them away, but I don't, do I? I spend the next eight days eating nothing but Chomps morning, noon and night and you just wonder, what was the point of spending a whole evening making my own Ferrero Rocher out of Ryvita and peanut butter so I wouldn't buy M&Ms at the cinema and blow all my syns for the week, if the week after it all goes to shit anyway when I gain three fucking stone eating nothing but Chomps. *All* because there's one night a year when I need to have enough chocolate to bolster the already loaded sacks of an indeterminate number of local children dressed as characters from films they've never even fucking seen, you know? Oh, you sleeping? You know we're landing soon? Bit of a pointless time to take a nap.'

You keep your eyes squeezed shut. The plane bumps along the tarmac and people in the cabin applaud.

Your mum is standing in Arrivals, holding a cardboard sign with your name written on it in her eyelash-delicate scrawl. The sight of her makes you want to weep. You push your suitcase with the broken wheel over to her and she wraps her arms around you. She gives you the parking ticket and her purse and she starts to manoeuvre your suitcase across the car park, the tendons in her narrow arms protruding.

When you finally took your A-levels, one year late, your mother drove you to and picked you up from each one, as though it were her failure to do so the first time that caused the problems. She only ever spoke gently to you about what happened that day, didn't ask too many probing questions. You understand that this was a triumph of will on her part. You wish you could apologize to her for not being normal and pretty and uncomplicated, for not being what she deserves.

You still haven't told her about what happened the night in the youth hostel, and you suspect you never will, for a number of reasons, but mostly because you think her knowing would be too exhausting for both of you. You also think it would be too easy for her to attribute all your failings to this one event, and you don't want to be absolved in that way – you know you were strange and wrong from the beginning.

The machine takes the ticket, and you feed four pound coins into the slot. It returns the ticket, and you follow the silhouette of your mother across the poorly lit car park. She turns back at one point and calls, 'All OK?' and the wind catches her short hair and gives her a wild quiff. You hope she knows it was nothing she did that made you like this.

Twenty-five years old – March 21st

The bell above the door dings. You don't look up – you continue arranging the plastic rack of cheap reading glasses. Some of them have silver chains and you display these ones more prominently. You think your favourite thing about working in the pharmacy is the slow and methodical arrangement of stock: reading glasses, anti-fungal socks, over-the-counter medications. If your supervisor isn't there sometimes you build towers and forts from Nytol. You have been working here for five months, since being handed your final cheque at the consulting firm, since giving up the struggles of the studio flat, since moving home, since asking your mother plaintively for help, since accepting the warm nurture of her concern. Your mother knows the pharmacy owner from church. She pleaded your case, said you were diligent and polite and capable of entering a 3-for-2 deal on all Dove products into a till.

The bell above the door dings again and then a minute later it dings a third time and this time you do look up. The woman glances around nervously before wandering to the haircare aisle. You stare.

She still has long blonde hair and the gap between her teeth. However, everything else about her is different now, softer now. The way she held herself at school always reminded you of the two-dimensional cardboard dolls you could dress with tabbed paper clothing. Now she's more like a watercolour, blurred at the edges. She's dressed in blue jeans and a short flowery top and she seems to radiate good health – she could be the face of probiotic yoghurt. She reads the back of a shampoo bottle and her lips move as she half mouths the ingredients. You haven't seen her in eight years.

'Charlie.'

She doesn't look up and you wonder if you imagined saying it.

'Charlie.'

She looks up and smiles absently.

'Hiya, I'm just browsing.'

You nod and she turns back to the bottles, picking them up in turn. Finally she picks a pink one that smells like raspberries and a dark-brown mascara and a box of tampons. She brings them to the counter and sets them down and takes a bit of paper out of her pocket and hands it to you. She says, 'Can I pick this up too, please?' It's a prescription for several types of medication you've never heard of. You look at her and she smiles serenely. You wonder what her abdomen looks like now.

'If you take this to the pharmacy desk back there, they'll fill it out for you – this is just the cash desk.'

Her smile sags a little at the edges.

'Oh. I thought I could do it in here.'

'You can, just not at this desk. The pharmacy desk is just back there.'

The smile regains its balance.

'Oh, great!'

She wraps her arms around the products, crumpling them and the prescription to her chest.

'You can leave the items here. I'll keep them if you want to go give the pharmacist the prescription.'

'Oh.' She doesn't move.

'You can pay for the items while you wait for the pharmacist.'

'Ohh.' She doesn't move.

'Here,' and you reach out your hands. She passes you the shampoo and the mascara and the tampons. She grips the prescription in one fist.

'So take it back there, and then come back here.'

She nods and walks away. A moment later she's back, smiling at you and shrugging.

'Sorry! Usually my mum gets it for me.' Her smile is enormous. She laughs and her hair twists and bounces around her shoulders. You think about how beautiful she is and then wonder at where the thought came from. You lean towards her.

'We went to school together.'

She peers at you. You wish you hadn't put her in this position. You try to arrange your face in contrition. You raise your shoulders.

'Yeah, sorry, it was a long time ago. I was friends with Rachael.'

'Oh yeah, Rachael! Of course I remember! Sorry – I'm not used to meeting people from school round here now, and you look so different. Sorry – bit slow!' and she thunks the palm of her hand against her skull and sticks her tongue out. You want to know what her breath smells like.

You put the items through the till and the total comes to £16.76. She scrabbles in her bag and you hear the low-pitched, strung-out 'Nooo' beginning in her throat. She looks up at you, and this time the laugh is remorseful. You thought you would feel angry. Instead, you realize you want to take care of her.

'I'm such an idiot – I did something so stupid.'

'Are you OK?'

'I forgot my wallet.'

'Don't worry – I'll sort it out.' You bring out your debit card and hold it to the reader and then look at your hands. They look like someone else's. You look up at her and she smiles the enormous smile again.

'Oh my God, thank you so much! You're a lifesaver!'

You don't say anything for a moment.

'It's OK.'

The pharmacist calls her name and she leaves the till. On her way out she turns and says, 'It was *so* nice to see you.' The bell dings and she's gone and you watch her through the window. She's trying to push the paper bag with the prescription into the plastic bag with the shampoo. She drops both. After she has picked them up she looks through the window and finds your eyes. She puts her palm to her forehead again and smiles. You smile back.

Twenty-five years old – March 22nd

She comes in again, wearing the same top but this time with a satin skirt that catches in the door. The bell dings as she opens it to release the hem and then dings again as it closes.

She walks up to the counter and smiles at you. She's having a party two days from now, wants to know if you'd like to come. She asks for your number and five minutes later you get a text: Hi! Its Charlie xxx

It's the first time she's ever texted you.

When your shift finishes that day you take out your phone and Google the name of each medication she's on. You use your employee discount to buy a pair of silver-chained reading glasses and three bottles of raspberry-scented shampoo.

Twenty-five years old – April

'It's such a cop-out though, isn't it? Any time I try to have a real conversation with him that's what he comes out with, "Oh Rachael, you're so beautiful. Oh Rachael, you mean so much to me." He might as well pat me on the head and give me a fucking biscuit.'

Rachael is sitting on the toilet in the baby-changing cubicle of the shopping centre. She and Greg now live in the city two hours away from you, are in the process of buying a house. Her pale-yellow and white striped knickers are stretched between her calves, and the naivety of her underwear seems dichotomous with her knowing what a mortgage is. Her thighs are spread and her arm is wedged between them and into the toilet bowl.

'Christ, it's difficult to actually get your piss on the damn stick, isn't it?'

You are sitting on the fold-down changing table, trying not to stare at her calves and the way her arm looks carved from stone. Your thighs melt wide over the table's padding – it's the same dirty cream shade as your skin. Rachael stands and straddles the toilet. She shakes her hips and droplets glitter down into the bowl. You look at the perfect rectangle of her pubic hair.

'Getting a good look, eh?'

You try to do a Russian accent. 'Such exquisite downy lady hair.'

She laughs. 'Here, take this, Vladimir,' and hands you the white plastic stick, one end dripping. You take it gingerly and lay it on the table next to you. You set the timer on your phone.

03:00

'I don't know why you wasted your money on those,' and as she pulls her pants up she nods at the box of two pregnancy tests sitting on the edge of the sink. 'You didn't even have sex with him.'

'I might have.'

'I think you might know.'

'I was drunk.'

02:14

'At what point, exactly, are you proposing you blacked out and let him shag you?'

'I don't know.'

01:57

'If you fucked him there would definitely be a fuck flash-back. A flashfuck!' She says this with delight. She flicks the elastic of her knickers against her ass.

'But I'm late as well.'

'The whole time I've known you you've had approximately eight periods. They're so rare they should be celebrated as a religious holiday. You're always late. I'm not even convinced you *have* a womb.'

'I have a womb.'

'It's a very sleepy womb.'

'A well-rested womb.'

'A womb with a view.'

'A womb-bat.'

She dances from one foot to the other. You watch the muscles in her thighs flexing and fading.

'Are you worried?'

'About this? Nah. I mean, I'm settled at work, the house is nearly sorted. If it's positive . . .' She trails off, wistful. Earlier, in the supermarket, she held a ham joint to her chest like she might breastfeed it. 'Maybe the timing isn't ideal, but I want kids, and I'm not having another' – she pauses – 'you know. So, if it's positive then Greg can decide if he's on board or not. For God's sake, he's almost thirty-three, and it's not like money's a problem for us.' Rachael's change of location has been accompanied by a promotion, and though she is never ostentatious with it, you notice that she always carries cash now, that her jeans are Levi's.

00:51

You squint your eyes and look at her.

'I can see you with a baby.'

'Right?'

00:19

00:18

00:17

00:16

Rachael nods once more at the box on the edge of the sink.

'Seriously, you're not going to bother with those, are you?'

'I just want to be sure.'

'I promise you, you little loon: you're not pregnant.'

00:05
00:04
00:03

She edges closer to the changing table.

'Can we look yet?'

Your phone vibrates like a pneumatic drill. You cancel the alarm. Rachael jumps up and down on the spot, flapping her hands in a way that makes them look boneless, like smoked salmon. You lift the test from its small, dirty puddle. You offer it to her.

'No, you look!'

You glance down.

'Negative.'

Rachael's hands grow bones and stiffen and she presses them to her thighs. Her jeans are still in a heap on the floor. For a few moments she doesn't speak.

'Oh well. Was a bit of a mad idea. Should probably wait a few years.'

'You OK?'

'Course! Weird I'm so late though.'

'Yeah.'

You dig your nails into the soft cushion of the changing table. When you take your hand away there are crescent-shaped indents. Rachael stands side-on to the mirror, her hands on her abdomen. The shopping bags sit in the corner, the ham poking out the top.

You picture Rachael and you, pushing buggies side by side in the park. People stop to look at what's inside. In your pram is the soft, frozen arch of a dead kitten; in hers is the pink ham, bound in green string. You coo at one another's monstrous children; the wheels roll smoothly over the footpath.

You shake your head to loosen the image. Rachael turns and grins at you.

'Well, go on then, crazy. Have your turn at Pregnancy Roulette.'

With a test still in its plastic sheath you jump off the table and move to the toilet. When you pull down your trousers you can smell the blood immediately. A long smear of dark red lines your knickers.

'Oh.'

'What?' Rachael turns and you tilt the gusset of your pants. You both look at the flat, dark dampness. She laughs and it sounds hollow. 'Oh. Guess that answers that, then. C'mon.'

She threads her wrists through the loops of the shopping bags, unclicks the door, walks out. You are still sitting on the toilet, the unused test gripped in one hand.

Twenty-six years old – June

Your mother takes you out for dinner on your birthday. She is thinner than ever now, and when the two of you are out together you wonder if, from the back, she looks like your child. You order tiramisu for dessert, ask her if she minds still having to look after you.

Her tone is gentle, deep with conviction. 'You don't stop being a mother, whatever it entails.'

Twenty-six years old – August

You wake to the sound of the smoke alarm and the feeling of clamminess on your forehead. You run your finger across your skin and it feels like recently defrosted meat. Your mouth tastes sticky and sour and you look over at the six Freddo wrappers on your bedside table. It's Saturday – your day off from the pharmacy. The alarm cancans in every room of the house. You go downstairs. In the kitchen Charlie is waving a tea towel in the air like a naval widow. She flings it wildly and knocks a Laos-shaped magnet and a photo of her and Katy, her girlfriend, riding scooters, off the fridge.

You have been living with Charlie for three months. For the first week you were tense, expecting to walk into your room to find her holding up a pair of your fraying mauve knickers, a fourteen-year-old's sneer on her face. 'You think anyone's going to want to fuck you in *these*?' It never happened though, and what's most unsettling is how unremarkable it all is; when you hear the bathroom door open and her high-pitched rasp say 'Shower's free'; when you come home from work to find her hunched on the sofa like a beautiful gargoyle, painting her toenails gold; when she forgets to wash her work smock and spends Sunday evening spritzing it with perfume and Febreze. She'll come to the pharmacy on days when you are working – sometimes to refill her prescriptions, sometimes to buy plasters or moisturizer for her dry elbows – and the two of you will walk home together. Charlie, who once loomed over you as some gorgeous Phobos, is actually just a person, and you're not sure if you're disappointed – how could someone so ordinary have reduced you to so little? – or relieved.

On the counter there's a baking tray covered in blackened hunks; on the stove is a saucepan full of hard-looking, singed rice. The tap is running, and water flows out of the sink and on to the floor. You twist it off and open the window. You lift a coat hanger from the table and use it to press the reset switch on the alarm. The silence aches for a few moments; like phantom limb syndrome. Charlie looks at you, rueful.

'Sorry.'

'What happened?'

Her brow furrows. 'I was going to make us curry.'

'Right.'

'That's what the rice was for.'

'OK. Don't worry – I'll sort it.'

'And the chicken.'

'Right.'

'It went a bit wrong.'

You lean back against the counter. The puddle on the ground nibbles at the edge of your foot.

'What happened to the chicken?'

'It burned.'

'Right.'

'I'm sorry.'

She says sorry in a way that is lilting and absent. It's as

though she's apologizing for your childhood pet having died – someone she didn't know, something that has nothing to do with her. You watch the puddle on the floor lose momentum. You shake your head.

'I'll sort it.'

'It was frozen. The chicken was frozen.'

'OK.'

'So I thought I would put the oven higher to defrost it.'

'Oh.'

'I was going to make curry for lunch.'

'OK.'

'And I was doing the washing-up.'

'Oh.'

'It all went a bit wrong.'

'I'll sort it.'

Charlie starts laughing, so you laugh too. She leans back on her hands, setting one hand on top of the steaming baking tray. She yelps and swears and jerks her hand away – the tray clatters. She inhales sharply and squeezes her hand against her chest. You gesture to the sink. She follows your hand with her eyes.

'I was doing the washing-up.'

'I know – I mean, put your hand under the tap.'

'I don't think there's room.'

You lift a couple of soapy plates out and stack them next to the sink. You gesture again and she comes forward and you turn on the tap.

'The floor's a bit wet.'

'It's OK.'

Charlie wanders out of the room. She's wearing fluffy bed socks that leave oval-shaped damp footprints on the

tiles. You take a sharp knife and begin chiselling the desiccated meat off the tray.

Later, after showering and brushing the chocolate stains off
your tongue, you come back downstairs. The air in the kitchen is still thick and smoggy. Charlie is sitting in the living
room, looking at her phone. She has used masking tape to
attach a bag of frozen peas wrapped in a tea towel to her
burned hand. It is enormous and pointed, like a lobster
claw. She waves it at you when you walk in.

'I thought this would help.'

'Right.'

'Sorry about the kitchen.'

'It's OK.'

You sit down next to her. Under your fingernails is black
with overcooked undercooked chicken breast. You pick at
it, casting flakes down on to the threadbare carpet. Charlie
is poking at the masking tape on her frozen-pea prosthesis.
You turn towards her.

'I could order us a curry if you want.'

She doesn't respond. The masking tape makes a noise like
a zip.

'Charlie.'

She looks up at you, holding her hand an inch away from
her face. 'Yeah?'

'I could order us a curry.'

'A curry?'

'Yeah.'

'When?'

'Now, if you want.'

'Oh.' She nods. 'Yeah – that might be nice.'

'OK, so what do you want?'

Charlie looks forward, then down at her towelled hand, then at her phone in her lap.

'Oh, wait. No.'

'What?'

'I'm going out, I think.'

'Oh.'

'It's Katy's friend's birthday.'

'OK.'

'She wants me to get to know her friends.'

'OK.'

'I can make you curry another time though, if you want. There's chicken in the freezer.' She pauses. 'Oh, wait.'

'Not any more.'

'Yeah.'

'It's with God now.'

She laughs. 'I will, though. I'll make you curry another time.'

'OK.'

'I should go get ready, I need to leave soon.'

'OK.'

Charlie gets up from the sofa and pads towards the door. She stops and turns back and you look at her.

'You all right?'

'Yeah' – a pause – 'Will you help me take this off?' And she waves the frozen-pea claw at you. Melted ice drips on to the carpet.

Twenty-six years old – November

'Nursing home' is the first thought you have as you stand in the living room, rotating slowly, looking at each corner in turn. The chairs seem unnatural, like they were designed for stiff joints and frail wrists. The curtains are chenille and floral, and on surfaces everywhere there are ceramic ornaments and framed photographs of your father and Janine: by the sea at sunset, red-faced and wearing shorts; astride bicycles in a park; sharing a pot of fondue with pints of beer. You think of one, or both, of them having to approach a stranger to ask to have these photos taken. Your shoulders seize up and go tense.

Your father calls from the kitchen, 'How many sugars?' and your voice comes out hoarse when you say, 'Three.' He replies, 'OK, sugarlump,' and then laughs to himself. Janine walks in with a plastic tray and three pieces of Victoria sponge. She smiles at you nervously, and for a moment she looks young. You suspect she went to a shop specially this morning, spent minutes in front of shelves, trying to choose which cake would alleviate the palpable tension of this situation. Your father appears, holding the door open with his foot and carrying another plastic tray. You wonder how many trays Janine owns, and if your father ever struggled to adjust to this new tray-filled existence.

You lower yourself into one of the reinforced, too-supportive armchairs, which holds you too far above the ground. You take a sip of tea and enjoy the syrupy aftertaste of slightly too much sugar. Janine smiles at you, and you think for a moment – before batting the thought away – that at least she got better at applying lipstick.

'So' – her voice is tentative – 'how's work?'

On the walk over from your mother's house you called Rachael and said, 'What if I put on a Scottish accent, or pretend to have a lisp, or occasionally meow?' She said, 'Why on earth would you do that?' And you said, 'She's never heard my voice, and I bet she'd feel too uncomfortable to question it.' Rachael said, 'OK, fine, but that doesn't really answer my question.'

'Fine,' you say now, in your normal voice, and when your father looks at you pleadingly you crumble the corner off your piece of cake and add, 'There's a lot of pleasure to be found in methodical stacking.'

Janine laughs nervously. 'Right,' she says, licking her lips.

'And I can get you a discount on compression socks whenever you want.'

She laughs again, and you resist the urge to ask if she has varicose veins.

You gesture at one of the photographs. 'Who took that, then?'

Your father visibly perks in his chair, and you find yourself smiling at his smile. He leans forward. 'Oh, this was great – there was this guy in a stripy top, a proper Frenchman, you know? And I go over and I say – and I don't know why it was me, Jan's French is a hell of a lot better than mine – and I say, "*Le photo, s'il vous plaît?*" and God, I sound like an idiot, and he says, "*Oui oui, d'accord,*" all cool and such, and he takes the camera and then says, "*Le boisson?*" and I just stare at him with my mouth open, and then he says again, "*Le boisson?*" and I can't work out what the hell is happening and eventually Jan says, "He's offering to hold your drink!" and so I give him my drink and he takes the picture and we say "*Merci merci*" and so on and he walks off and then I turn and I say – get this – I say, "I was about to tell him we didn't want any fish!"'

Janine is laughing into the back of her hand and quivering on her seat. Her other hand is on his knee, which bounces up and down frenetically. He is struggling to breathe through the force of his laughter, and you try to imagine your mother in Janine's seat, giggling delicately. You realize you can't. When his breathing returns to normal he wipes his cheeks with his fingers and looks at you. You smile wanly, and he blushes. He takes a sip of tea and you administer cake on to your tongue, dropping crumbs into your lap. You can hear the sound of a lorry outside, backing up.

You want to make things easy for him, but you don't know how. You wonder if this is how your mother felt at the beginning of their lives together. You look around the room again, notice a DVD boxset on the table. You nod at it. 'Any good?' and he follows your eyes. 'We haven't started it yet,' he says, 'but I've heard it's a lot like their other one – the one on the ranch?' You nod, and say, 'It was great,' and his tone is hopeful when he says, 'Shall we give it a go?' You say, 'Let's do it,' and he passes you the box while he fiddles with the DVD player. You rip the plastic open with your teeth. He takes the disc from your outstretched arm. 'Thanks, love.'

Twenty-six years old – January

'What were the flowers like?'
   'Why do you give a shit about the flowers?'
   'I don't know.'

Rachael is climbing into the bath. Her hair is wrapped up in a towel – it points upwards like a Whippy ice cream or a conch shell. She puts her phone inside a mug – *Everyone is entitled to my opinion* in purple lettering – on the bath's edge.

'Any song requests?'

'"Riders on the Storm".'

'Jesus – where did that come from? You're such a little weirdo.'

'You asked.'

'Well I guess that's my bad, then.'

You sit on the closed lid of the toilet, your feet up on the edge of the bath. Rachael pokes one with a soapy finger. She adopts a placatory tone.

'The flowers were, I don't know, normal. Yellow, pink, purple. Happy flowers; big fat blooms. Some tulips and then something else. I don't know much about flowers.'

You picture Bethany, swirling and radiant and egg-coloured in her meringue dress, her big cheeks flanked by big yellow tulips. You wonder if she remembers sitting in the park, her rosary beads catching the sun. Rachael tickles the sole of your foot and you jerk it away.

'I really like "Riders on the Storm".'

'Fine, OK. I'll put it on.' She wipes her hands on her towel hat and sidles over to one side of the bath. She taps at her phone and you look at the wide expanse of puffy, salmon-coloured skin on either side of the toenail on your big toe. A month after you didn't take your A-level history exam your mother took you to a podiatrist – a young woman with a ponytail who said, 'Call me Carol.' She injected the skin with anaesthetic and then hacked at the nail, at the nail bed. She extracted a thick blade of diseased flint from inside your toe: it was dark yellow and grey and you could smell it. Your toe wore a helmet of bandages for six weeks – you had to wear a rubber sock to take showers. When the bandages came off the nail looked strange and shrivelled and small. It still does. Rachael turns and looks at it too.

'It never really went back to normal, did it?'

'No.'

'God, that was a rough year for you, wasn't it?'

'I suppose.'

'And yet here you are!' Rachael blows chunks of bath foam at you. 'As normal and as healthy as we all could have wished!'

'Yeah,' you say, and you take a scoop of foam and mime licking it. Rachael laughs. She reaches over and opens and closes her fist like a toddler. You lift the joint that is sitting on the back of the toilet. You light it, inhale, then pass it over. She sucks on it, leans back.

'So, speaking of normal and healthy, how is it?'

'How's what?'

'Don't play all coy with me – how is it living with your former aggressor turned winsome dependant?'

'You mean Charlie?'

'No, I mean the nebulous but ever-present awareness of your own mortality. Jesus, of course I mean Charlie.'

'It's OK.'

'I never thought I'd see the day you two would be living together.'

'Yeah.'

'Well, except maybe when we were, like, fifteen – then I could have seen you living as her indentured servant.'

'Yeah.'

'You get a bit of a kick out of it, don't you?'

'Out of what?'

'Having her at such close quarters, all vulnerable.'

'No, I don't.'

'You totally do, you little freak. Is it a power thing?' She pauses, then whispers conspiratorially, 'No, no, wait – is it a *sex* thing?'

'No.'

'I love it. I always knew you were a dark little saucepot.'

'Did Bethany look good?'

'If you're so curious, why didn't you just come?'

'I wasn't invited.'

'You could have been my plus one.'

'That would have been weird.'

'Well, you could have been Charlie's plus one, then.'

'It's weird she was invited.'

'Sunday carvery religion, remember?'

'Oh. Yeah. Mini sausages and profiteroles religion.'

'Yorkshire pudding and gravy religion.'

'Paper hat and roulade religion.'

'Loading your handbag up with orange jelly religion.'

'I never liked orange jelly.'

'Don't let your ancestors hear you say that.'

'What jelly did you like?'

'Oh, I only ever ate transubstantiation jelly – Jesus-flavoured.'

'Yum.'

'But to circle back, Bethany has always first and foremost worshipped at the altar of Charlie.'

'She said she had a good time.'

'I take it she didn't tell you what happened.'

'What happened?'

'Well, if you think being my plus one would have been weird, then I don't know how you would have coped with the weirdness of me chasing Charlie through the reception with a towel because she started having her period through her skirt.'

'No. No, she didn't.'

Rachael passes the joint back to you and pulls her knees to her chest. The corners of her mouth stretch from one end of her face to the other. A cluster of bubbles hangs off the diamond on her engagement ring. Greg proposed to her on New Year's Eve in an Italian restaurant. He paid a waiter to film it.

'Yep, it was terrible, and also kind of hilarious, and also kind of sad. She started talking about the break-up and then she proceeded to get completely fucking wasted.'

'She still seems pretty upset about it.'

'Yeah. Who would have thought a little thing like diminished cognitive function would be enough to stop Charlie having a girlfriend.'

There is silence and you rub your palm up and down the dark bristles on your shin until your hand feels hot and itchy.

'I always wondered . . .'

'What's that?'

'Did her girlfriend get paid a stipend?'

Rachael yelps. 'Nasty!' But she doesn't stop smiling. She

lifts up another mound of foam and blows it at you. 'Are you getting in or what?'

You put the joint out in the sink. 'I guess.'

'You going to keep your knickers on again?'

'Yeah.'

'Why do you do that?'

You think of all the dark poisons swimming around inside you, turning circles in your lower abdomen, your crotch. You shake your head.

'Just.'

'Weirdo.'

The faucet digs into the space between your shoulder blades. You arrange the foam so it hides the bulges on your torso. Rachael is drying her hands on her hat again.

'So, how's your job?'

'Your tits turned out really great.'

'I know, right?'

'Do you think that's why he proposed?'

'Fuck off.'

You picture Charlie, a Red Admiral butterfly opening its wings on the pale fabric covering her ass cheeks. You feel a rush of affection, and guilt. You should say something kind about her, but the moment has passed. Rachael holds her phone high above the surface of the water. One breast points at you and you search the skin for the dotted line of where the nipples were reattached.

'Any song requests?'

'Can we have "Riders on the Storm" again?'

'Actually, you know what? Thank *God* you weren't at the wedding.'

'Did they play "Riders on the Storm"?'

'Of course they didn't.'

'I guess "Lady in Red" might have been more appropriate.' Another pang of guilt.

Rachael snorts with laughter. Her towel comes loose and lands heavily on the surface of the water. 'Oh! Fuck!' She peels it off and drops it on the bathroom floor.

'Do you think Greg will mind us having baths together once you're married?'

'Somehow I think you sitting in our bath with your knickers on will be the least of our problems.'

'It's a really nice house.'

'Right?'

'Are you going to try for a baby?'

'Anything but that.'

The water is murky and dark green with bath gel. Your limbs float in the khaki-coloured nether space, and it looks like your legs are missing below the knee.

'Can I come to the wedding?'

'Of course you're coming! Don't be stupid. In fact, if you move down here I'll make you help me plan it.'

'Will you play "Riders on the Storm"?'

'As long as you promise not to bleed all over the dance floor.'

You tilt your head in mock-contemplation, then arrange your face in mock-reluctance. She laughs, and looks down at her soft, inflated breasts. You straighten your leg and poke the underside of one with a pointed toe. She squeals.

'Ew! Don't touch my lovely fake boobs with your weird toe!'

'Rachael?'

'What's up, buttercup?'

'Is it true Charlie lost her virginity when she was fourteen to a stranger outside a club?'

Rachael screws up her face. 'Is *that* what people said? God, I'd forgotten about that. I hope not, that would be too fucking depressing.'

Twenty-six years old – April 20th

It's 2:15 a.m. and you are stumbling home from the pub. There was a night out to celebrate one of the male pharmacist's birthdays. Josh. You spent most of the evening trying to position yourself so that your knee could touch his under the table without it seeming deliberate. The others are going to get chips and kebabs but you know that Charlie was going to a party tonight – her first since Katy broke up with her – and you're worried she might have left her key in the lock or her straighteners on. The house is in darkness and the keyhole is empty. You wonder about going back to try and meet the others, to try and resume pressing your thigh into his while talking to someone else. You don't have his number, so you send him an email and then sit down on the front step. You hadn't wanted to appear overdone so instead you felt uncomfortable all night in your loose, grubby t-shirt, hands constantly trying to improve your flat, greasy hair. After fifteen minutes of your phone staying silent, you give up and go inside. You get into bed without brushing your teeth or washing your face.

★

You wake up at the sound of the front door slamming and Charlie's uncertain and heavy footsteps on the wooden floor. You check your phone – it's 4:10 a.m. You open up your email inbox – nothing. You read the email you sent.

Hey I want to come back where have you guys gone is there going to be an after party? Hope you had a really good birthday. Best xx

You let out a low groan. You wait for the sound of footsteps on the stairs before trying to go back to sleep. When they don't come you sit up. You wonder about sending a follow-up email. You call out 'Charlie?' and hear nothing. You get out of bed and feel about on the floor for your pyjama bottoms, using your phone screen as a torch.

When you go out on to the landing the house is still in complete darkness. You say again, softer this time, 'Charlie?' Still nothing. You go downstairs, unable to resist playing with the sticky, clumped-togetherness of your hair at the scalp. You walk into the lounge and see a person-shaped smudge with its back to you. It is then you hear a soft, persistent trickling sound, and as your eyes adjust you see the pants stretched tight between Charlie's knees as she squats and pisses into the corner of the living room. The carpet is thin and not absorbent enough to stop the piss spreading out in tendrils across the floor. You inch over to the sofa and sit down, pulling your feet up under you. After a long time the sound stops and you say, 'Charlie,' and the figure turns and wobbles. You lean over and turn on the lamp and both of you shield your eyes with your hands for a moment. Charlie's eyeliner is smudged down her cheeks and one eyelid is half down as she peers at you. She lowers herself to the floor, falling heavily on to her hip. Her black and white skirt has ridden up and you can see the dark-pink softness between her thighs.

'You OK?'

She takes a moment, like the words are being built letter by letter on her tongue. When she speaks it is slurred and loud.

'I just – I don't – where—' She stops and presses her finger-tip into the dark streak on the carpet emerging from underneath her. 'I thought – I thought this was—'

'I know. It's all right. I'll sort it.'

Her eyes, one still only half open, turn wet and red and her mouth begins to curve downwards. She sniffs violently. She rubs her eyes and spreads the black further across her cheeks. One set of fake eyelashes has come half loose and drifts in front of her eye like a windscreen wiper.

'I really – I – I miss her.'

'I know.'

'I thought that was going to be it, that – that we were going to be together.'

'I know.'

She leans wildly on the heel of one hand and pushes her-self up. She waves gently from side to side, like wheat in a field. She wanders towards the door.

'I'm – I'm sorry – I thought this was—'

'I know. It's OK. Go to bed.'

She stumbles upstairs and you hear her bedroom door closing. You sit and stare at the hand-shaped stain on the carpet. You lower yourself to the floor, just in front of where one of the stain's promontories stops. You put the tip of your finger to it and it feels for a moment like someone has poured cold water all over you. You shiver and then you turn and look out the window; it's still dark, it won't get light for another hour. You take your phone out of your pocket and check your inbox: still empty. There is an ache above one of your eyebrows so pronounced and localized you think if you took a kebab skewer and pushed it in, hard, the pain would stop. You pull your knees to your chest and press your forehead against them. You bury your hands in your hair and moan softly into the folds of yourself. At 5 a.m., you go back to bed.

Twenty-six years old – April 29th

You quit your job and tell Charlie you are moving out. She hugs you and you hug her back tightly, feeling the way she moves along with your deep breaths. You never brought up how she treated you at school, and neither did she. After all, is there anything more worthless than exhaustive remembering? What good has it done you?

Two hours later she has found someone to take your room, and you are delighted not to have inconvenienced her. You buy an extra suitcase and you are surprised by how easy it is to fit your life into two fabric rectangles, although you leave behind your saucepan and your two plates and two bowls and your assortment of cutlery. You find a room to rent in a flat with two strangers in their early thirties. You apply for three jobs.

Twenty-six years old – May

You have breakfast with your mother the day you leave. She orders porridge with fruit and you order pancakes with bacon. At the bus station she holds you for a moment and tells you to stay safe. You feel a familiar hot pressure below your eyes. You tell her you will, because who is worth staying safe for, if not her? You fight the urge to apologize for a hundred things she has probably forgotten about. She puts a white envelope with money into your pocket and helps you manoeuvre the two suitcases on to the bus. She waves to you from the kerb as you board. You wave back.

You take a window seat, looking at yourself in the glass. Your reflection is crowded; as the bus moves, your face houses a yard of coaches, the river, a furniture showroom, a Domino's pizza, an old quarry. Soon, vast spaces of countryside and hills roll faster and faster across your features. You watch as this small portion of the world moves through you. You get a text from Rachael saying Can't wait to share a city with you, sweetums! and another text, from your father, saying SAFE JOURNEY LOVE! KEEP IN TOUCH XX. You wonder if any good decision can exist in a vacuum.

Twenty-seven years old – November

'Well, what do you think?'
   'I think my head looks too small for my body.'
   'You're an insane person.'

The light in the changing room is softer than you're used to, and you like how it gently blurs the mottles of your body. The dress is dark red with long chiffon sleeves and a low back. You slide open the curtain. Rachael whistles.

'Well, aren't you a foxy little minx?'

'A foxy little minx with a small head.'

'I think minxes – *minxi*? – have quite small heads anyway.'

'So we could argue it's a deliberate aesthetic choice.'

'Provided there was a scenario in which we had to argue in favour of your head looking too small.'

'So you *do* think my head looks small?'

'Shut up, minxy.'

You drag the curtain closed and pour yourself back into your jeans. Rachael told you to wear clothes that were easy to get in and out of, so that morning you had put on tracksuit bottoms and a jumper, then changed into jeans and a t-shirt, then changed into a skirt and tights and a jumper, then changed into chinos with a swimsuit underneath, then back into jeans and a jumper. The bridal shop is warm, and the underarms of your jumper already smell like a fridge after a power cut. You leave the changing room. Rachael is sitting on the sofa, eating M&Ms. She raises her eyebrows.

'Well?'

'I don't think so.'

'Not to worry – plenty more dress fish in the dress sea.'

Rachael already has her dress – it was the first one she tried on and she looks impossible in it. You go to a rail and start flicking. She comes and stands next to you.

'So, how's work?'

You shrug.

'That bad?'

'It's not bad. It's furniture.'

'What's furniture?'

You smile. 'The soft bits for the man houses.'

'Ahhh, the fabric solids for the sitting and the laying.'

'The small squares and the bigger squares.'

'The ecru squares and the taupe squares.'

'You've learned so much here.'

'Right?' She laughs. 'But yeah, so it's not exactly scintillating?'

'I spent an hour and a half yesterday helping a woman choose between a twenty-three-inch pouffe and a twenty-four-inch pouffe.'

'Pouffe-ing hell.'

'Right?'

Rachael brings out a dark-blue dress with a high neckline and inspects it. You look at it over her shoulder. You poke her in the side.

'What's up, snookums?'

'Do you remember that girl who came to give us a talk in school?'

'I'm going to need more specifics.'

'She wore a tartan skirt and a turtleneck – she went to uni somewhere posh, Bath or Newcastle or Exeter or something.'

Rachael frowns at the dress. 'Vaguely.'

'She was really pretty.'

'Was she?'

'She had nice hair and big shoes.'

Rachael's brow clears. 'Oh! Allie . . . something.'

'Was that her name?'

'Yeah – she was a few years above us. God, that speech she gave was such bollocks.'

'How come?'

'Well, she said all that stuff about struggling in school and not having friends or passions and all that shit.'

'Yeah?'

'It was all shite – I asked about her afterwards and turns out she got amazing grades and was on the hockey team and in the choir and pretty much, like, everything. She was a big fucking golden goose of a girl.'

'Really?'

'Yeah – I don't know why the teachers let her get away with all that social outcast shit. Her big toe probably had a more deeply entrenched sense of belonging than any of us.'

'Not like my big toe.'

'God, no. Your big toe had self-esteem issues and agoraphobia.'

You continue to stare at the dress. It has black beading around the neckline, like constellations, or buboes. 'I wanted to be her, for a while.'

Rachael returns the dress to the rail. 'Seriously? Even with those *shoes*?'

Twenty-seven years old – November

'May contain trace amounts of nuts,' you mutter into the fridge, holding the pot of hummus up to your eyes.

'What?' The voice arrives soft and sudden from an

unforeseen orbiter at your right shoulder. The pot hits the floor with a hollow *thwap* noise.

'Shit – sorry.' The voice is female. You turn and see a girl with red lips and a septum piercing setting a glass down by the sink. You pick up the tub and return it to the shelf with the plastic carton of button mushrooms and the plate with half a pink steak, sweating under the blue fridge lights.

'That's OK.' You keep your gaze angled forward. You sense her edge closer.

'Would you mind? Mine's the white.' She gestures and you pass out the bottle of Sauvignon Blanc with the £6.99 label still on. 'Thanks.'

'No problem.' You try to foster an environment in which she feels safe to leave.

'So,' she says, leaning against the counter, 'how do you know everyone?'

The house is loaded with brushed chrome and letter-shaped bookends and fluffy pillows. There's a chin-up bar installed in the doorframe of the spare bedroom and a book about succeeding in business in a wicker basket next to the toilet. The house has recently been bought by two people named Jon and Caoimhe, colleagues of Greg's. Caoimhe is dressed entirely in camel. She greeted you at the door with, 'I love your shoes,' and then showed you where to put them: 'We're a no-shoe household. Like in Japan!' The party guests seem a disconcerting mix of high-earning adults who look like they have gym memberships and beautiful twenty-somethings making corduroy glamorous.

You talk directly to the girl's septum piercing. 'Greg brings me along to things for two reasons.'

'Oh yeah?'

'One' – you bring a bottle of lager out of the fridge and examine it – 'to appease Rachael.'

She smiles. 'OK.'

'And two' – you pick at the label with your fingernails – 'for sporadic and unexpected comic levity.'

She lets out a laugh. 'So you're the entertainment value?'

'You bet,' you say, and you turn and toss the bottle out the open window. There's a brittle rustling noise as it lands in one of the globe-shaped shrubs. The girl puts her hand to her mouth and exhales in multiple short puffs. Her eyes are wide. 'Holy shit,' she says. You gesture to the window. 'I should probably go get that,' and you leave through the back door into the garden.

When you come back you are surprised to find she is still standing there. She reaches out a hand and you give her the beer. She puts the rim of the cap to the edge of the kitchen counter and slams her palm down on top of it. The cap pops off with a lip-smacking noise. She gives it back to you.

'Thanks,' you say. The beer is cold and bready.

'Good?' she says, rotating her wine glass between her two hands. Her fingernails are long and painted pale grey.

'Lager's a drink of diminishing returns,' you say.

She raises her eyebrows. 'OK?'

'By the time you reach the end of a bottle you're really not enjoying it any more, but you persevere. It's like . . .' and you pause. You're feeling drunk, bold, detached from yourself. 'Anal sex, I assume.'

She laughs hard, and you realize that she is someone who

is generous with her laughter. You wonder if this means she is kind, or just naive. She asks, 'What's your name?' and when you tell her she brings out her phone and wiggles it at you. You type in your number and hand it back. She looks you up and down.

'I like your top,' she says.

'No, you don't.'

More laughter. 'I do. It looks nice on you.'

'No, it doesn't.'

Upstairs there is the sound of a door slamming. Your eyes go upwards.

'Sounds like someone else is having fun too,' she says.

You look at her. 'Are you having fun?'

'Aren't you?'

'Yes, but I thought it might be one of those Mandela Effect moments.'

She laughs. 'What's that?'

'You know how a lot of people think Nelson Mandela died in prison?'

She takes a step closer. 'I'm going to need more information.'

'Well—'

'Hey,' a new voice, 'can you come upstairs?'

Greg is in the doorway, his shirt sleeves rolled up. You look at him. You look at the girl with the septum piercing. She keeps her eyes on you, steady. You set your beer on the counter.

Rachael is bent over the toilet bowl, curled and drooping like an orchid. The sink has two inches of ochre-coloured vomit in it.

'Hey, buttercup,' she croaks when she sees you. 'Clean up in aisle me.'

'She won't let me near her,' Greg says from the doorway, his hands in his pockets.

'Fuck you, daddio.' She balances her forehead on the toilet seat.

He sighs. 'Yeah, great, thanks. Nice one.' His tone is like vinegar.

You gesture with your head for him to leave. He closes the door and you turn on the tap. The water comes out fast and scalding. Steam rises with the smell of cooked carrots and rotten eggs. 'Shit,' you say, and turn it off. You look at Rachael, 'I think I made it worse,' and she laughs at the floor. You put your fingers in the water and squeak at the cold burn of it. Rachael leans back against the bath and watches, her cheeks smudged with black, as you use a steel toothbrush holder to scoop the poisonous soup out of the sink and into the toilet. She coughs, belches deeply. 'You're a real problem-solver, aren't you?'

You wobble on your feet. 'I should have been a Girl Scout.'

'Abso-fucking-lutely.'

You flush the toilet and sit next to her on the floor. The armpits of her silver top are dark with sweat. After a moment she says, 'Greg's gonna be pissed off tomorrow.'

'He'll get over it.'

'He might call off the wedding.'

'He won't.'

'He might.'

'He won't.'

'I guess.'

Your phone buzzes in your pocket. You ignore it and lean forward, taking a book from the small white end table loaded with potpourri and tea lights. You open it.

'Want to hear an inspirational quote?'

She closes her eyes. 'Sure.'

The letters worm across the page. 'Climb your mountains. Eat your demons.'

'What?'

'Be the horse you want to see in the world.'

She groans. 'Stop it.'

'Sprinkle the salt of your dreams on the slugs of your enemies.'

'You're an idiot.'

'A woman should have two things: confidence and a sandwich toaster.'

'That's the one. I feel much better.'

'Good.'

She leans forward and puts her head on her knees. You move your hand in circles over the thin, clammy fabric of her top.

You take out your phone to call a taxi while she sprays herself with deodorant and perfume, purloined from the cupboard over the sink. You have a text from an unknown number:

Thanks for the unexpected comic levity xx

You stare at the screen. 'I didn't know people still bought Lynx,' Rachael says.

You look up. 'It's the fragrance of champions.'

'Or the fragrance of ass-hat solicitors.'

'Tomato tomato.' You say 'tomato' the same way both times.

'How long on the taxi?'

'Five minutes.'

'Beautiful.'

'Shall I go get Greg?'

'No. Tell him to stay and get off with someone with a functioning womb and their own pair of tits.'

She looks at you. Her eyes are unreadable. You mime contemplation. 'Bit of a mouthful.'

She smiles. 'Maybe just tell him to stay and have fun then.'

'Less creative.'

'Tell him to stay and dry-hump a vacuum cleaner.'

'Perfect.'

You lean over and kiss her on the forehead. She flaps the fabric of her top like a bed sheet and groans. 'Ugh, sorry I'm such a mess. Did you have a good time?'

You think for a moment about the girl's long, pale fingernails. Your phone vibrates again and you think the thought away. 'Taxi's here.' Rachael cups her hand over her mouth and breathes out, sniffs, grimaces.

You bow to her as you open the bathroom door. 'Let's ride, cowgirl.'

Twenty-seven years old – February

Your mother sends you a text with a screenshot of a job listing. This, maybe? She does this about once a month. You are sticking new price labels on top of old price labels on bed sheets. The furniture shop is air-conditioned, even though outside it is cold and sharp and the dead leaves crunch underfoot like cornflakes. A young mother comes in with two small children on leashes. One child knocks a ceramic hedgehog off a shelf and its nose snaps off. The mother is apologetic and tired-looking and you consider not charging her for it.

As she hands you the money – 'God, it's dear in here, isn't it?' – your phone buzzes with another message from your mother. **Molly had the baby. Little girl. Aoife. Joan isn't thrilled about the name.** The door swings closed behind the second child and a breeze rustles the tea towels on the rail. One, printed with an aerial view of the Hebrides, falls to the floor. The shop sits, empty. You read the job listing.

Twenty-seven years old – April

You emerge from the examination room with a circular, tan-coloured plaster in the crook of your arm. Rachael is sitting in the waiting room, reading Henry James. You sit down next to her.

'So?' she says.

'If I haven't heard anything in two weeks it means I have the all-clear.'

'You won't hear anything.'

A part of you has always known this. 'Yeah,' you say. 'Probably not.'

'But I guess it's not really about that.'

You look at the plaster – the skin around it is lilac. 'Yeah.'

She puts her hand on your knee. 'I'm glad you told me, snookums.'

You take a deep breath in and it feels as though your lungs have been sitting empty for hours. You exhale. 'Yeah?'

She squeezes. 'Yeah.'

Outside the clinic, she reaches into her bag and brings out a packet of chewing gum. You take one and shatter the coating.

'Pub?' you say.

'I'm not sure,' she says. 'Now that we've got that out of the way I wonder if we should just keep doing practical things.'

'Dental check-up?'

'Hair trim?'

'Dog grooming?'

'Where would we get the dog?'

You gesture at a chocolate Labrador across the street. 'There's one.'

'Lot of hassle, stealing a dog.'

'True.'

For a lot of your life you have been struggling against the force of the secret inside you. You take a few steps in the direction of the city centre, and you feel something akin to lightness, freedom; there is a newly vacant place in your mind for new thoughts to grow. For the first time since you were seventeen, it feels like the handbrake is off.

★

It starts to rain, and Rachael grimaces up at the sky. 'Forget the dog. Shall we go to the pub?'

A raindrop lands in your eye. You blink rapidly. 'Yeah.'

'Perfect.'

Twenty-eight years old – August

The fluorescent light above you flickers. Will, the sports editor of the Sunday paper, pushes himself away from his desk on his wheelie chair, calls across to you, 'Aaaand done.' You laugh placidly, keep your eyes on the screen. You are proofreading a feature about a stained-glass artist. You Google the word 'bokeh', then bring out your phone. You text your mother: New word alert: bokeh.

She replies after a few minutes: Good one, although sounds like something a bit unsavoury.

You reply, I ate too much cake and I bokeh-d.

She replies, Charming!

You put your phone down and turn back to the screen. The artist mentions a film-maker, and so you Google 'Jerome Hiler', make sure the spelling is correct, that the ideas and work attributed to him are accurate.

The newspaper's offices occupy the ground floor of a building that also accommodates another newspaper, a film company, a solicitor's office. The windows stay open permanently and you can hear cars rattling the manhole covers on the road outside. You are on a team with two other proofreaders and fact-checkers, and your focus is on finance, features and obituaries. You'll often text your mother words you don't recognize: 'tragus' or 'fungible'. You love the quiet of the job, reading the short messages people have written about their dead loved ones: 'Grandmother to Ciaran and Niamh'; 'Much cherished by children Frank and David'; 'The family would like to extend their gratitude to the staff in Ward 20'. You love the dimly lit office and the water cooler and the staff noticeboard with offers of spare rooms and guitars for sale. You love the specificity of your job – its low-key, noble duties. You change 'practise' to 'practice', do a find and replace.

The sports editor approaches from behind. 'You sticking around a bit longer?'

You flinch – you'd forgotten he was still here. You rotate to face him, steady your voice. 'Yeah, for a bit.'

'Give that thing about Joyce a once-over, would you? My head's fried.'

'I will.'

He smiles. 'You're a dream. See you later.'

'Bye.'

Once he's gone you slide your shoes off and fold your legs under you on the seat. You pull yourself on four wheels, via desks and door handles, to the kitchen. You stretch your lips around four custard creams and wheel yourself back to your desk. You eat one of the biscuits and put a few missing apostrophes into the final paragraph. You hear the rain start – droplets bounce off the tilted window and speckle the carpet. You put another biscuit in your mouth, upload the piece to Google Drive. The clock in the corner of your screen changes to 20:00. For a moment you think about oblivion, but then you stop yourself. You open up the sports feature.

Perhaps living contentedly is just finding pursuits that distract you from thoughts of oblivion. It occurs to you that everyone else probably figured this out long ago. You pick up another biscuit. You hum.

Twenty-eight years old – September

Rachael and Greg's first dance is to 'Songbird', performed by a string quartet made up of Rachael's prepubescent cousins. You stand at the edge of the dance floor, watching them. Your dress is floor-length, and black, which is unconventional, according to your mother. You also suspect it is the most inexpensive item in the room. However, this morning, as Rachael's aunt helped you with the zip and flipped the fat, artificial waves of your hair around your shoulders, you looked in the mirror and felt something like acceptance – 'OK,' you thought, as you made eye contact with yourself. 'This is OK.'

Your maid-of-honour speech took the form of a fake obituary, listing Rachael and Greg's future happiness as past events. In your vision they die seventy years from now in a meadow, surrounded by grandchildren and rabbits and squirrels. Rachael's mother frowned throughout.

The song stops, and they kiss, and you clap. The DJ appears, and you hear the first bars of 'Riders on the Storm'. Rachael looks around and summons you to the dance floor with a pantomime finger. When you reach her she throws her arms around you. You shout the lyrics at one another and sway violently.

Bethany was invited, but couldn't come. She is a primary-school teacher now, somewhere just over the border, and has two young children. You never contact her, although you do still sometimes wonder if she was happy at school – despite both being on the periphery of the same group, you realize that you never knew much about her, and you never tried to know much about her. Charlie wasn't invited, and when Rachael said, 'She's *your* friend, not mine,' you were surprised to realize that she was right. Charlie now co-manages the upscale salon by the river, and her blonde hair sits around her collarbones in a thick, blunt cut that makes her look like a Scandinavian architect. She is engaged to a woman called Emma, who is less attractive than you would have expected, but more intelligent. When you visit home you often meet them for coffee – Charlie has been sober for two years, has become vocal on social media about substance abuse and mental health – and Emma will sometimes rest her hand on Charlie's hand, or press her forehead into Charlie's shoulder. You think Charlie is happy, and you like that you don't begrudge her that happiness. You think sometimes about how important it once seemed for all of you to get away from here.

You are staying at your mother's house tonight – when you sleep in the small single bed of your childhood you often wake up convinced you are fourteen again. Tomorrow you will meet your father and Janine for lunch before getting the bus back. The two adults you live with are now in a relationship, and often you will all have dinner together before they disappear to their now-shared bedroom. You like them, and they seem to like you, although you're not sure how long they will tolerate your encroaching on their future.

After 'Riders on the Storm' you go to the restroom. The sensor-operated flush goes off mid-piss, and you mutter 'Fucking fuck sake' as you dry your ass and the backs of your thighs with toilet paper. You walk out on to the hotel patio, where you are suddenly as ostentatious as a time traveller among the non-wedding guests dressed in their jeans and t-shirts and sandals. There is a man on a bench. He looks up when he sees you. He smiles.

Twenty-eight years old – December 5th

The Christmas tree is about the height of a toilet. It is fluffy and fibre optic. You spread out its branches with your hands, place it in the corner, plug it in. The white clusters interspersed among the fake firs become blue, then purple, then pink, then red, then orange. You put the small gold star on top and stand back for a moment to watch. You take your cactus off the windowsill and carry it to the sink, run cold water on its soil, let it drain. You switch the kettle on.

Your new flat is small, but bright. It has a bedroom, a bathroom, a kitchen, and at night you can hear the hailstones bouncing gently on the fire escape. You put three mounds of sugar into the cup, add the teabag, the water, three centimetres of milk. You lean back against the kitchen counter and make the outer edge of your foot line up with the fake-tile print on the linoleum. The tree reinvents itself every few seconds.

Twenty-eight years old – December 13th

'I think they should make a musical out of *The Crucible*.'

He laughs. 'I would go see that a hundred times.'

'Right?'

The sky is clear and unusually starry. He tops up your wine glass and thinks for a moment.

'In my school production of *The Crucible* a lot of the kids got cast as mice.'

'I didn't know there were mice in *The Crucible*.'

'It was a fairly unfaithful production.'

'Who did you play?'

'I can't actually remember.'

'Did you play the crucible?'

He laughs. 'I probably played a butter churn.'

'You'd make a very handsome crucible.'

'I could wear pantaloons made of a sort of dense, heavy clay.'

'You wouldn't be able to dance in them.'

'Oh, the crucible wouldn't dance – it would just sway authoritatively.'

'I always wanted to write a musical about Shergar.'

'I think there would be a market for that.'

'Would you like to play Shergar's front end or Shergar's back end?'

'Oh, back end for definite.'

'Someone could say, "Are you Shergar?" and then the front end could say, "We sure are." That's it. That's all I've got.'

He laughs again, his full lips retreating to reveal big white teeth, a few of which are missing corners. You laugh too, tentative, and you don't say anything when, a moment later, he looks at his watch.

This is what you know about the man you met the night of Rachael's wedding: you know that he is ten years older than you; that you find him handsome in a way that seems implausible, that even when you see his reflection in the chrome kettle in your apartment, or in the black glass pane of a taxi going through a tunnel, he is still beautiful. You know that when you are not with him you search for his face in supermarkets or at tables in restaurants or among the extras in a television show. You know that after this he will come back to your apartment, that the Velcro between your legs will slip open to let him in, and afterwards he will put his arms around you and the cold air in that chasm inside you will turn warm, for a moment.

You also know that he won't stay over – he will order a taxi, will return to the home he shares with his wife. Even in the certainty of this, there is a kind of comfort. Rachael refers to the relationship as your 'daddy-issue starter kit'. You call it 'an anthropological experiment', and saying this almost seems to negate the ramifications of what you are doing. He is teaching you how to be half loved, how to defer entirely to another person's whims and desires and schedule. You suspect this will prove useful, later.

'I think we have time for one more. Another drink, gorgeous?' He smiles at you.

You look into his eyes. Every moment with him feels like a junction. You nod.

Twenty-eight years old – January

Happy New Year! Your mother.

HAPPY NEW YEAR, SWEETIE! Your father.

Happy New Year, gorgeous. Hope you're having the best night. Your boyfriend who is elsewhere, spending the evening with his wife. You reply to him first, then you message your mother: Happy new year, pal! Her reply comes quickly.

Coming home soon?

Yeah – after chips.

Chip fiends.

I think you mean chip friends.

Call if you can't get a taxi.

Will do.

Don't walk!

We won't.

Enjoy chips. HNY to Rachael.

Rachael reappears with two shot glasses. 'It's like Helmand up there.'

'I thought I could smell mayonnaise.'

'Here you go, sweetums. To youth!'

'To youth.'

The dark liquid tastes like hot Listerine. You love the feeling as it cauterizes your throat. The Deer's Leap is transformed on New Year's Eve – all around you is light and noise. The band starts up and the crowd centipedes towards the music. A man bumps into you and you recognize him: Jordan. He once sat behind you in French class, next to a girl called Sinead who you heard was addicted to heroin for a while but now studies Theology. Jordan would

230

make a show of rolling the words so aggressively in his throat that you could hear the phlegm gathering. He wore non-regulation trousers and had black hair with a spiral shaved into one temple. He puts his lips to your cheek, then your ear, slurs, 'Happy new year, sexy.' You say, 'Thanks, you too,' and he says, 'And who might you be?' You can't contain the force of your laugh – how would you answer that question? You make a shooing motion with your hands, then turn away. He shuffles on. Rachael produces a glass of red wine and you take turns to drink from it.

Twenty-eight years old – February 11th

Your thick-soled boots chew up the stones on the path. The headstone is subtle and black with gold lettering; your uncle's plot neighbours are an eight-year-old child and an elderly married couple. Your mother arranges the wreath with gloved fingers.

'Looks good,' you say.

She nods. Her irises are so pale they are almost see-through. She says, 'You get a lot of your personality from him, you know.'

You scratch at one wrist. 'Yeah?'

'Yes. I used to not know where you came from, but now I can see it. It's not your father, or me. It's him.'

A red, blocky 4x4 squeezes through the cemetery gates. A woman in knee-high rubber boots sets a fat pug on the ground. You watch it waddle, bow-legged, towards a plot.

It sniffs at the flowers. A part of you urges it to lift its hind leg and do some anointing.

Your mother doesn't look up from the grave. 'He was a slow-burner too.'

You take your eyes off the pug. 'Oh?'

'Yes. Took him a while to figure things out.'

'Probably not as long as me, though.'

She laughs. 'It's not a contest.'

'But if it was.'

'Well, yes' – she adjusts her bag on her shoulder – 'if it was, you might win.'

'That can be my yearbook award: most likely to succeed long after everyone has stopped caring.'

She nudges you. 'Not everyone. Not me.'

The woman is trying to clip a leash to the pug's collar as it struggles between her shins. 'Must be exhausting,' you say.

She laughs again. 'But worth it,' she says, 'in the end.'

'Hope so.'

'Are you hungry?'

'A bit.'

'Let's go.'

'OK.'

Twenty-eight years old – May

The ultrasound doesn't look much like anything, you think.

'It doesn't look like much, I know,' Rachael says, as Greg waves it at you expectantly.

'No' – you pause – 'it's a very handsome blob.'

Rachael laughs. Greg takes it back, looks at it, frowns. At the bar representatives from two rival hen dos are battling over the last bottle of on-offer prosecco. It's 4 p.m. on a Saturday, and you're not sure why you chose this bar, which has an ornate front and is a honeytrap for tourists. You like being here with Rachael and Greg, though. What once might have made you feel lonely now makes you feel solid and consequential. They are an entity, beautiful and established, and you are welcomed as an addendum to that. How worthy must that make you?

'So,' says Rachael, 'fancy being godmother?' and Greg groans – he wanted pageantry. You take a large mouthful of beer, swallow it, then mime bolting from the booth. They laugh. You wait another moment, then shrug, and say, 'Sure.'

'Great,' Rachael says. 'I mean it's really a meaningless figurehead position, godmother.'

'No, it's not,' Greg says.

'I think she's right,' you say. 'I've heard it's mostly appearing at public events and wearing a sash.'

'Sometimes a tiara,' Rachael says.

'I don't think the godmother ever actually meets the baby,' you say.

'The godmother gets a photo once a month,' Rachael says. 'It's like sponsoring a snow leopard.'

Greg balances his chin on his hands and waits. Rachael nudges him. 'Don't pout.' She turns to you. 'He's just oblivious to the realities of godmotherhood because his godmother spent most of his twenties trying to take baths with him.'

You nod sympathetically. 'You poor thing.'

'No no, he liked it.'

'Is his godmother pretty?'

She makes her eyes lusty. 'Smokin'.'

You lean across and pat his arm. 'Don't worry, Greg, I promise to take plenty of baths.'

Rachael laughs. 'With the baby?'

'With Greg.'

Greg murmurs into his hands, 'I hate both of you,' and Rachael puts her hands to the still-invisible swell of her lower abdomen. 'Don't let blob hear you say that.' She takes a mouthful of Pepsi, then looks up again. 'So, how's Mr Monogamy?'

You look down at your drink. 'Oh, that ended.'

Her eyes go wide. 'Shit.'

'Yeah.'

'Shit.'

'Yeah.'

'When?'

'Two weeks ago.'

'Shit.'

'Yeah.'

'Did you . . . ?'

'Yeah.'

'Whoa.'

'I know.'

Greg moves his eyes from you to Rachael to you, a spectator at a tennis match. 'Guys,' he says.

Rachael takes a breath and breaks the rally. She reaches across the table. 'I'm sorry, buttercup.'

'It's OK.'

Greg leans forward. 'It was' – and he pauses – 'complicated, though, right?'

Rachael smirks. 'Oh, listen to him; he's so coy.'

'It was complicated,' you say.

'And unsustainable,' Rachael says.

'Yeah.'

Greg says, 'So why'd you go along with it?'

'Because it was good at the time.'

He says, 'That's not a good reason.'

Rachael says, 'Sure it is.'

'No it's not,' he says.

'It's just like our marriage—' Rachael starts, breaking off when she sees his expression. For a moment her laughter eclipses all other sounds in the pub. The belligerent hens glance over.

'It had to end,' you say to him. 'But I enjoyed it for a while.'

'And how do you feel about it all?' Rachael says.

'OK.'

'You sure?' she says.

'Yeah,' you say. 'I'll be OK.'

She smiles wider, and the edges of her mouth strain to touch the bar on one side, the wall on the other. 'Yeah,' she says, 'I know.'

Outside, you inhale wetly on your cigarette – a habit that seemed like a good alternative to apples. Across the street people emerge from the bus station, ungainly with coats and suitcases, the way you did two years ago. You squint at them in the caustic light. The door opens next to you and Rachael emerges, putting on her sunglasses.

She punches you lightly on the upper arm, 'M'lady,' and

you drop your cigarette and grind it into the pavement with your foot. She says, 'Don't do that on my account.'

You look at her, dismayed. 'I wouldn't dream of smoking near my beloved godchild blob.'

'You big softie.'

You say, 'I take my duties very seriously,' and she nods. The unexpected gravity of the moment makes you want to put a wet finger in her ear. You look at your reflection in her honey-tinted lenses, then turn back to face the street.

You are twenty-eight, one month away from twenty-nine. You don't own a beige pantsuit and there is nothing to suggest the world is about to end. Nothing but your own sporadic sadness, which is sometimes heavy as a duvet and sometimes, like now, barely there at all. Rachael leans against your shoulder and the two of you watch the cars go past.

Your phone vibrates in your pocket. Rachael says, 'You're popular,' and when you show her that the text is from your father she laughs. She says, 'Another beer?' and you nod and she goes inside. You reply to the text and then scroll through your inbox. You find the log of old messages between you and the older man with the beautiful smile and the beautiful wife.

Him: I love you.

You: I love you too.

You concentrate on keeping your tears glued to the red triangles of your caruncles. You delete the messages, then you delete his number. When both are gone you resume breathing and scrolling. You pause at one from six months ago: Thanks for the unexpected comic levity xx

A car horn wails and you look up to see a woman darting across the lanes of traffic in suede wedge heels the colour of a cartoon dolphin. She stops in front of the pub and glances up at the facade. She says, 'All right, love,' before continuing down the street. You smile at her, at her bare back, goose-pimpled and the colour of cinnamon. You look at your phone once more before putting it away and opening the door. Noise and warmth find you. You wonder what happens now.

Epilogue

Eleven years old – August

'Did you give David the money for the lessons?'

This is the first thing your mother says to you when you arrive home. You swap your grassy trainers for the blue, pillowy bedroom slippers sitting at the front door. It is the last week of summer – on Monday you will have your first day at your new school. You are excited for this section of your life to start, for new parts of yourself, new friends and abilities. You are taking tennis lessons, because the school has two tennis courts, terracotta and austere.

That morning your mother handed you a brown envelope filled with ten pound coins – the fee for the next week's sessions. Walking through the park you decided to take a shortcut to the tennis courts through the wet, poorly drained marshlands. The pointed corners of the envelope dug painfully into your side, and so you ripped it open and trickled the coins into your pocket. You didn't notice them jumping and sliding out of the white mesh lining of your shorts.

You admit to having lost them – a rare moment of impulsive honesty. There is a rapid turnaround, a sudden change in mood and temperature. You are hurried into the back seat of the car and then your mother is leaning over you to make sure your seat belt is fastened – an act of tenderness that seems inconsistent with her anger. Then you are being pulled along by one arm through the park. The friction in the air builds as leaves rub against leaves and your thighs rub against each other. You gesture, not to the wide, tarmacked footpath, but into the shady greenery of the soggy woodland.

'Silly girl, why wouldn't you just take the footpath?'

The sun is out. Flakes of it filter through the damp trees. You and your mother squelch around in the saturated earth, looking for the coins. Your mother tells you things about yourself: you need to learn the value of money; you need to learn there isn't an infinite replenishment; you need to grow up; you need to think.

Every time a coin is found you feel her anger dissipate slightly. When you find the fifth you even allow yourself to shout over to her in celebration. She smiles wryly and replies, 'Good. Keep looking.' You leap over a deep trench, filled with brown water. When you hit the earth on the other side there is a viscous, phlegmy grunt from the mud. You look down at your feet. They are still clad in your blue, pillowy bedroom slippers. Your mother hadn't noticed, and you hadn't said anything. The soft fabric at the edges is almost black and your white socks inside are turning a muddy grey colour. When you slide your heel out you see the insole is glistening, soaked through. You ease your foot back in. You stare at your feet in their wrong shoes, surrounded by lush, verdant grass. They look so comically wrong, like something you might circle with red pen in a Spot The Difference puzzle: a snowman missing an eye or a house missing a door.

Twenty minutes later your mother will concede defeat at five coins. She will have found three, you two. She will call for you to stop looking and when you reach the tarmac she will notice your feet, drenched in their soft cotton coracles. She will say, 'Why on earth didn't you change your shoes?' and you will not have a response. She will sigh a sigh so heavy it will seem to shake the low leaves on the trees. Once you are reinstalled in the back seat she will peel the shoes and socks off your feet. The socks will be put in a bin in the car park and the shoes will go into a plastic bag and into the boot. She will say on the drive home, 'I don't understand you, sometimes,' but her tone will be soft and you will see her smile in the rear-view mirror. When she stops at the supermarket for milk she will bring out a Freddo bar and carton of Ribena. You will slurp it noisily for the rest of the journey home.

That will all come later, though. Right now you are still standing in the park. Your mother is some distance away, hunched over and searching. The dark mud, asleep under the grass, is like slow-acting quicksand. You watch as the black saturation at the base of your slippers spreads upwards. A pillar of sun lands on the top of your head. It makes the pale skin on the backs of your hands glow – the veins look like watermarks. You keep your eyes fixed on the ground; fixed on your wrong shoes. You stay standing like this; your head downturned like a broken sunflower. You smile.

Acknowledgements

I am incredibly grateful to the Arts Council of Northern Ireland, particularly Damian Smyth, for a General Arts Award that facilitated the writing of *Tennis Lessons*.

This book could not have happened without:

Sophie Scard, my agent. Alice Youell, my editor, and the wonderful people at Doubleday. My mum, my dad, and my brother, James. Tara McEvoy, Michael Nolan and Kevin Breathnach. Catherine McFadden, Linzi Hamilton and Manuela Moser. The writers and tutors at Goldsmiths College and the Seamus Heaney Centre. The vital friendships I have found in Derry, Belfast and London.

Thank you all for your continued tolerance, and for making me a better writer.

Susannah Dickey grew up in Derry and now lives in Belfast. She is the author of three poetry pamphlets: *I had some very slight concerns* (2017), *genuine human values* (2018) and *bloodthirsty for marriage* (2020). Her poetry has been published in *Ambit*, *The White Review*, *Poetry Ireland Review* and *Magma*, amongst others. In 2018 she was shortlisted for *The White Review* short story prize, and in 2019 she was the winner of the Vincent Buckley Poetry Prize. *Tennis Lessons* is her first novel.

Pill   28-05-21

PILLGWENLLY.